" His name was

3/2/2011

Philip Cavern

A BUFFALOPE'S TALE

By the same author

A BUFFALOPE'S TALE

Philip Caveney

Book Guild Publishing
Sussex, England

First published in Great Britain in 2010 by
The Book Guild Ltd
Pavilion View
19 New Road
Brighton,
BN1 1UF

Typeset in Palatino by Ellipsis Books Limited, Glasgow

Printed in Great Britain by CPI Antony Rowe

A catalogue record for this book is available from The British Library.

ISBN 978 1 84624 563 3

For the many readers who have asked me how Max came to be so miserable – this book is for you.

Chapter 1

The Great Migration

For as long as I can remember, I have always stood out from the herd.

That is to say, from the very beginning, I was different from my fellow buffalope. I didn't really *look* any different from the others and, I'm sure, my habits were more or less the same as those exhibited by buffalope the known world over. But I had something that none of the others seemed to possess: an enquiring mind. It was this, more than anything else, that led me to become the creature that I am today, admired and revered across the known world as Max the Mighty.

My earliest memories are of being with the rest of my herd on the great plains of Neruvia, and of being very close to my Mother, who, for the purposes of this story, I shall call Bess, as this is a name you humans will understand and it's the closest-sounding human

1

name I can find to her real one, which is achieved by expelling air through the nostrils. But I can hardly expect mere humans to master that technique; it's all some of you can do to have an intelligent conversation in your *own* language.

Bess was kind and attentive, quite the nicest mother a young buffalope could wish for, and she was always standing guard over me, keeping an eye out for trouble. Even now, if I close my eyes, I can still feel her great damp snout snuffling at me in the night and I can taste the sweet, rich milk that she gave me whenever I was hungry, which, if I am honest, was most of the time. I've always had a healthy appetite, which is why I've had such problems maintaining my figure over the years.

My Father, who I shall call Dan, was a great hulking presence in my life, always on the lookout for predators and other dangers. I remember his huge curving horns and the big shaggy shape of him and, though he rarely exchanged more than a few words with me, most of them pretty stern ones, it was certainly comforting to have him around.

Now, I could tell you loads of stuff about the buffalope life, but really it mostly came down to this: through the spring and summer, we stood around and ate grass; lots of grass; lots and lots of grass. The stuff was virtually coming out of our ears.

And when autumn came creeping in, relentless winds blasting cold rain across the hills, it was then that the great migration would begin.

It happened every year at more or less the same time. Melchior, the herd's leader, would sniff the cold air with his nostrils. He would glance at the ancient sage bull, Lazarus, his most trusted advisor, and then he would lift his head and issue a great trumpeting bellow, which was the signal for us all to stop doing whatever it was we were doing and start migrating. Countless hooves would stir into action and we would be off, with a sound like rolling thunder, across the vastness of the plains.

In those far-off days there must have been near enough a thousand of us. When danger threatened, the whole herd would break into a gallop and, when we did, the plains would shake beneath the force of our hooves. When we couldn't run, the adult animals would form a protective circle around us youngsters, their mighty horns lowered to present any attacker with a circle of deadly grey spikes that only the most ravenous beast would dare to chance.

The migration was long and arduous and we were heading South West to the hills of Torin, where, in a hidden valley, lay The Grove: a sacred place of sanctuary, known only to us buffalope. It was widely

3

believed that The Grove had been bequeathed to the herd by the great buffalope god, Colin (again, the closest human name to his real one, which is made by making a deep grunt and adding a high-pitched whinny at the end). It was said that Colin had broken off a small piece of his own heavenly home and let it drift down to the earth. Mind you, even then I was not entirely convinced of the existence of Colin.

The world was supposed to be hung from his nostrils on a great silver ring and, to be absolutely honest, I couldn't quite see how such a thing was possible. The plains were massive and they were only a tiny part of the known world, so it seemed to me that the world itself must be immense and surely there could be no snout in existence that could carry such a weight?

Lazarus was always telling us young buffalope stories about Colin and saying that we should be pure in heart so that when we passed over, we would go to him in the great wallow in the sky. There were many in the herd who claimed to have seen him, galloping across the clouds at sunset, but I put that down to them eating too many of the strangely shaped mushrooms that sometimes bloomed on the plains.

In Torin, on the Western coast of the known world, the weather stayed more temperate and great orchards of pommer trees grew wild. We could feast on the windfall fruit right through the autumn and into the winter and, even then, amidst the roots of the trees, we could still nose out wild vegetables, grasses and lichen. Meagre pickings, to be sure, but through the warmer months we had built up great reserves of fat, enough to see us through until next spring, when, once again, Melchior would give his call and we would begin the journey back to the plains.

It was the buffalope way of life, sure enough – but, even at that tender age, I was beginning to be irked by the inevitability of it. I had taken part in the great migration only twice in my young life and I was already getting well and truly fed up with it. For one thing, my hooves ached something terrible. It's been a life-long problem for me, one that nobody ever seems to take seriously. But I'm telling you, after days of marching across that blooming plain, they were killing me.

For another thing, it was boring going through the same routine, year in, year out. I was longing for a bit of variety in my life. There's no harm in that, surely?

As soon as I was able to talk – which, I confess, did not take me very long, I was forever asking my poor mother tricky questions. I well remember one particular day, when we were browsing as usual in the midst of the herd and I felt that I simply had to have an

PHILIP CAVENEY

answer to a problem that had been perplexing me for ages.

'Mama,' I said. 'Why do we make the great migration every year?'

'My dear,' Mama said, 'we do so because the rest of the herd do; and they do so because Melchior, our esteemed leader, says that it is time for the journey to begin.'

'Yes, but it's very hard on the hooves, Mama. It's not nice having aching legs. Sometimes I swear my hooves feel as though they are about to drop off. Why must we be forever trooping up and down?'

'It's just the buffalope way,' said Mama.

'That's no explanation,' I complained. 'You might as well say, because the grass is green! Here's an idea for you. What would happen if we decided to stay here on the plains?'

'You'd starve to death,' said Papa, who was a buffalope who didn't like to use any more words than were strictly necessary. 'Or you'd freeze.'

He was browsing a particularly lush bit of grass at the time and didn't really want to be disturbed by my childish questions.

'There wouldn't be enough grass to feed an entire herd through the winter,' added Mama.

'Yes, but it wouldn't *be* the entire herd, would it?' I

persisted. 'The rest of them would go thundering off and we'd have whatever was left all to ourselves. There's only the three of us, we'd be laughing.'

'Not when a pack of lupers came after us,' said Papa gloomily. 'And started ripping us limb from limb.'

'We could take care of *them*,' I said dismissively, tossing my underdeveloped horns this way and that. 'What are lupers but mutts with an attitude problem?'

I must confess that I already had a vastly inflated opinion of my own abilities.

'There's safety in numbers,' grunted Papa. 'Now belt up and let me enjoy my dinner.'

He let out a great gust of wind from his rear end, just to make sure I fully understood that as far as he was concerned, this was the end of the matter.

A word about wind. I appreciate some of the more delicate amongst you humans will doubtless be raising your eyebrows at the very mention of such goings on, but let me assure you that to creatures that dine daily on acres of grass, the expelling of loud gusts of wind is an inevitability. Indeed, amongst buffalope, such a process has been raised almost to the level of an art form. Why, in our herd alone, I can recall certain buffalope who could produce notes, sound effects and even short pieces of music from their back ends. But I'm getting off the subject.

Papa moved away a bit. Mama gave me a consoling snuffle with her nice wet snout.

'You're only a youngster,' she told me. 'There's no reason to worry your little head over things you don't really understand.'

I felt like telling her that I *did* understand, only too well, but Papa was still close enough to give me a whack with the edge of a horn, so I kept my peace. But I felt sure, even then, that I wasn't going to put up with this migration business for very much longer.

Chapter 2

Pestilence

As it happened, the matter was soon taken away from me. It was high summer and I was just at the beginning of my third year, when the great pestilence came upon the herd and changed our way of life forever.

Let me warn you now: this part of my story is not exactly a laugh riot. If you're the sort who finds sickness a problem, skip on a chapter or two. Those of you who don't mind shedding a tear, get your kerchiefs ready.

I can remember the very day it started. I was playing with Luthor, a nice but rather dim fellow of around the same age as me. In many ways, he was my best friend. We were practising our head butts, something that buffalope are extremely good at and spend a lot of time trying to perfect.

Under the proud gaze of our respective parents, the

two of us would stand facing each other a good distance apart and we would snort and stamp our feet and generally make a lot of noise. After a while, we would run at each other and bash our horns together with a hideous clacking sound, almost knocking ourselves unconscious in the process. Then we'd stagger away, shaking our heads to try and dispel the dizziness, before facing up to each other and going at it again.

Yes, I know, a pointless exercise. In fact, I seem to remember thinking that very thought, but I was only doing it to please Papa, who seemed to set a lot of store by this kind of stuff and wanted me to grow up to be a big, tough customer, just like him. Anyway, Luthor and I were just lining ourselves up for the next bash when, suddenly, a frightful bellow filled the air and we all turned to look.

We saw that one member of the herd, a rather skinny and moth-eaten old chap whom I shall call Angus, was staggering towards us looking very distressed. As he drew nearer I saw that his eyes were all red and filled with pus and that thick saliva was dribbling from his open mouth. A mantle of black flies buzzed continually around his head and he was making sounds of distress ... no actual words, you understand, just a hideous bellowing as though he was in great pain.

'What's wrong with Angus, Mama?' I asked. 'He

looks a bit rum, if you ask me.' But she just shook her head.

'Come away from him, dear,' she said, and I could hear the note of fear in her voice. 'He doesn't look at all well.'

'No, he doesn't,' I agreed. 'Do you think he's eaten a bad mushroom?'

As we watched, appalled, Angus's front legs seemed to buckle beneath him and he crumpled untidily to the ground. He lay there roaring and moaning and, pretty soon, a group of buffalope were gathering around him, nudging him with their snouts and asking him stupid questions like, 'Are you all right, Angus?' I ask you, did he look like he was all right? I took a step towards him, intent on asking a more sensible question, like, 'Where does it hurt?' but Papa's voice halted me in my tracks.

'Stay away,' he told me. 'I've seen this before. He has the pestilence.'

'What's that when it's at home?' I asked, mystified.

'It's a bad thing, little one,' said Mama. 'A summer sickness. If you catch it, you die.'

'What?' asked Luthor, in his slow-witted way. 'You mean, like *really* die?'

Papa gave him an annoyed look.

'Of course,' he said.

But Luthor still wasn't getting the message.

'No, but, like if you get it, you'd be ... dead?'

'Yes,' growled Father. 'Is there something about the word "die" that you don't understand? You would fall sick and you would drop dead, very soon afterwards. So stay away from him. And tell everybody else you meet that they should do the same.'

Luthor nodded. He seemed to have understood. He trotted back over to his parents to tell them the news. I looked at the great press of buffalope standing around Angus and I felt a twinge of worry go through me.

'*They* aren't exactly keeping their distance,' I observed.

'More fool them,' said Papa. 'Come on.'

And he led us through the herd to stand on the outer edges of it, as far away from Angus as was possible without actually leaving the safety of the herd.

It was a blazing hot summer that year. The grass grew dry and yellow, like wisps of straw and in places the parched earth broke open in great jagged cracks.

The next day, we could hear the bellows of other stricken buffalope coming from various places in the midst of the herd. News travelled like wildfire from creature to creature.

'Harry has the pestilence, now! Bertha is sick! Edward isn't feeling too clever!'

I tell you, it was enough to make you feel very gloomy about the future. I've never been very good with sickness. If somebody starts throwing up, I'm out of there like a shot.

Melchior passed word among us that each morning we were to move away to new pastures, leaving the sick and dying behind us. He warned us that no matter who fell ill – mother, father, sister or brother – they were to be left well alone.

As the days passed, the situation got steadily worse. More and more of our number succumbed to the sickness and as each successive beast fell prey to it, the herd would move off to a safe distance, leaving a series of shaggy heaps lying in the grass behind us, at the mercy of the carrion beasts of the plains. Vultures and buzzards filled the sky and packs of wild mutts closed in for the kill. Even as we walked away, we could hear the anguished roars of those we had left behind, as hungry jaws got to work on them.

I could see what the herd was trying to do, but it quickly became clear to me that we would never be free of the sickness as long as we stayed together. The pestilence was hopping gleefully from one shaggy body to the next. Moving away when a creature was actually displaying symptoms of the illness was leaving things far too late. The next morning, I tried to explain this to my parents.

'If we stay with the herd, we are history,' I told them. 'It's as simple as that.'

'But what else can we do?' protested Mama. 'Being with the herd is the only life we know. To strike out on our own would be too dangerous.'

'Not as dangerous as staying with the herd,' I assured her. 'They are dropping like flies out there. I'm telling you, we've got to break away.'

'But what of the predators?' asked Papa, who, for once, was actually taking me seriously. 'The lupers and panthers . . . I cannot hope to protect you both on my own.'

'Papa, we will have to take our chances,' I said. 'Unless you want to end up like the others. And besides, I can give any predator that comes after us a jolly good thrashing.'

Papa eyed me doubtfully.

'You couldn't thrash your way out of a ruddy pommer orchard,' he said disparagingly. 'You're not even fully grown, yet.'

'I'm big for my age,' I said, defensively.

Then we heard a commanding call from Melchior. The herd leader had walked up onto a small hillock and was gazing sadly down at the buffalope all around him. I saw with a twinge of fear that his eyes too were red and filled with pus, and I heard Papa take a sharp intake of breath as he noticed this.

'Creatures of the herd,' said Melchior, and his once steady voice sounded weak and faltering. 'This will be the last time I speak to you. The sickness is upon me. I feel it coursing through my veins. Lazarus will act as leader now, until you appoint another to take my place. You must leave me now and move on.'

At this there was a great outcry from the herd. Everybody loved Melchior and nobody wanted to turn their backs on him. But he was adamant.

'If this herd is to survive, you must go on your way and leave me. I want nobody to approach me as you go. Please, this is my last request of you. I go to join our fallen brothers and sisters in the Great Wallow. Farewell and good luck to you all.'

Reluctantly, the herd began to move away, our heads low as a mark of respect to the buffalope who had led us so well for so long. As I went by, I sneaked a look at Melchior. He was standing alone on the hill, his nose nearly touching the ground and I could see that his legs could hardly hold him upright, but he was grimly hanging on until we were all out of sight.

I learned in that moment what true courage really

was, and I hoped that the stories of Colin and the Great Wallow were true. I did not want to think of Melchior ending his days as nothing more than a carcass rotting under the glare of the sun.

We continued to move across the plains and, after a few days, more than half of our number had died. I began to plead with my parents, telling them that, if we didn't break away now, it would be too late for us. Finally, even Papa had to concede that I was talking sense.

'I hate to admit it, but the lad is right, Bess,' he said with a sigh. 'We're doomed if we stay. We'll slip away tonight. But we must do it quietly. If others see us going, some are sure to follow.'

Bess simply nodded. She had always obeyed her husband in such matters and even her fear of leaving the protection of the herd couldn't overrule that.

When the sun went down that night, we made sure that we were browsing on the very edge of the herd. From the midst of it came the by now familiar anguished bellows as more creatures succumbed to the sickness. Finally, when it seemed that most of the buffalope around us were asleep, Papa gave an almost imperceptible nod and we began to move quietly away from the others.

Papa had decided to head in the direction of Torin

and The Grove – though we knew it was way too early, he had surmised that, by the autumn, those of the herd that had survived would make their way to this familiar place and we would meet up with them again. We moved as silently as we could but we hadn't gone very far when I heard the sound of hooves behind us and when I looked back, I saw my regular playmate Luthor, trotting after us. I turned back to look at him.

'Where are you going?' he asked excitedly.

I looked into his nice but dim face and tried to think of something I could say to him. Obviously, I couldn't tell him the truth.

'We're just going . . . for a walk,' I said.

'Great, I'll come with you. I'll just go and tell Mama and Papa . . .'

'Er . . . no!' I said, perhaps a little too sharply. I knew exactly what would happen if I let him do that. The commotion he would make would wake up other members of the herd and then they'd want to come and, the next thing you knew, the whole lot of them would be trooping after us, completely defeating the object of the exercise.

'It's er . . . it's a bit of a *secret* walk,' I said.

'A *secret* walk?'

He looked somewhat confused by this and I couldn't blame him. I wasn't entirely sure what it meant myself.

My mind was going ten to the dozen trying to think up a plausible explanation.

'Er . . . yes, we're going to a secret place to . . . er . . . find a cure for the sickness. You see, I had a dream . . . and in the dream, Colin told me . . .'

Luthor gasped.

'You have talked to Colin?' he whispered. 'The great buffalope god, Colin?'

'Er . . . yes. Well, *he* spoke to *me*, actually. I just listened. In the dream, he told me that if I went to a certain place and ate some . . . umm . . . special blue fruit . . . it would cure the pestilence that afflicts the herd.'

'Oh boy! Colin said that?' Luthor was getting very excited now, wheeling this way and that on his spindly legs. 'I can't wait to tell the others!' he cried.

'Yes . . . I mean, no! No, that's just the point. You mustn't. Colin said I was to mention it to nobody, otherwise the cure wouldn't work.'

Luthor looked crestfallen.

'But you've told *me* now,' he said. 'Does that mean that I've ruined it?'

'Er . . . I don't think so. No, what he actually said was, I was to tell nobody except my very best friend. Yes, that's what he said. And that's you, Luthor, so it won't harm the plan. But you see, the blue fruit is some distance away and we don't really know how long we'll be gone. So you must go quietly back to the herd and mention it to nobody. Do you understand? And . . . if anyone asks you if you've seen us . . .'

'I'll say that I certainly didn't see you creeping away in the night.' He nodded his head. 'In that direction.'

This didn't sound too promising, but there wasn't much I could do about it.

'Well, Luthor, you'd better get back to the others,' I said, 'before you're missed.'

'I suppose so. What a shame I can't come with you. It sounds like a real adventure.'

'Yes . . . still, see you later, eh?'

He nodded. He looked so trusting that I felt horribly ashamed of myself and almost relented and told him that he could come with us but, just then, Papa appeared at my side.

'We must be going, son,' he said. 'Time's moving on.'

I nodded. I gave Luthor a stern look.

'Remember now,' I told him. 'Not a word.'

I turned and walked away. After I'd gone a short distance I stole a glance over my shoulder and Luthor was still standing there, watching me leave with that same trusting expression on his face.

I often wonder what happened to him after that.

Perhaps the pestilence claimed him, as it took so many others of the herd. Perhaps he grew up, found a mate and sired many young calves. I will never know, for I never saw him again. I sometimes dream of him though, standing alone on the plain beneath the vastness of the night sky, gazing after me with those big, trusting eyes.

I would like to see him once more before I die so I could tell him that I'm sorry for tricking him the way I did. I hope it wasn't too long before he realised that I wasn't coming back.

Chapter 3

Out From The Herd

When the sun rose, the three of us were quite alone on a vast stretch of plain. We looked in all directions but could not see any sign of the herd. It felt strange to be out on our own: scary, yet, at the same time, exhilarating. We began to amble in the direction of Torin, taking our own sweet time and stopping to graze whenever we felt hungry, which, with buffalope, is most of the time.

Papa was very nervous about this. I can't say I blame him. He and Mama had spent their entire lives with the herd, so for them to leave its security must have been an awful wrench. In those first few days, Papa was very watchful, always lifting his head to look in all directions and he advised me to be the same. I wasn't about to argue with him.

Once, I spotted a distant pack of lupers racing across the plain.

'Look at them,' I muttered. 'Running along on their back legs and howling at the sky. Just who do they think they are?'

'They're the most fearsome predators on the plains,' Papa told me. 'Let's not forget that, and let's just be thankful they're not heading our way.'

'Huh. They don't scare me,' I said.

But the truth is, they terrified me. I had once seen a pack of them attack an old bull that had fallen behind the rest of the herd and it was one of the most awful things I'd ever witnessed. Mind you, I was young then. I didn't realise that there were worse things than that in the world.

At night, we would find what little shelter there was on the plains and we would huddle together for warmth. Mama and Papa would press in protectively on either side of me, and Papa somehow managed to keep waking every so often to gaze slowly around and snuffle the air, searching for the tell-tale scents that would warn him of any predator that might be lurking in the shadows. I felt safe and secure in the midst of my parent's shaggy coats and was able to sleep soundly, never waking until the sun rose.

As the days passed and no harm befell us, we all

began to relax a little. Of course, we missed our brothers and sisters of the herd, but we only had to think about how many others must be dead by now to realise that we had made the most sensible decision.

'You know, we might have started something here,' I told my parents, as we ambled along one day.

'Whatever do you mean?' asked Mama.

'We've changed the way things have been for ages. I mean, the herd has been together for as long as anyone can remember. Nobody ever stepped away from it. But now we're saying, "Hey, buffalope, it's all right to be on your own." We're trendsetters, that's what we are!'

'The boy's brains are addled by the sun,' said Papa, despairingly.

'No, but think about it, Papa! We're out on our own and we're doing fine, aren't we? Nothing terrible has happened to us. It's all right to break away from the herd.'

But I had spoken too soon. It was on the morning of the fifth day, that something happened that would change my life forever. Even now to speak of it fills me with an overpowering sense of dread. And, believe me, if you thought the last bit was distressing, you've heard nothing yet.

It happened unexpectedly. I was grazing contentedly on a patch of dry grass, when Papa lifted his head and stared back in the direction we had come from. I turned to look and saw that there was a great cloud of dust on the horizon. We watched for a moment in silence and then discerned that some animals were approaching us at speed. It was their feet that were kicking up the dust.

'Lupers?' I asked anxiously, my former bravado quite vanished.

Papa shook his head and snorted.

'Equines, I think.'

'They are no danger to us,' I said.

'*Wild* equines are no danger,' said Mama. 'But sometimes they belong to the Uprights.'

The Uprights. I had heard other buffalope speak of them with dread in their voices. The Uprights were tall, thin creatures with little or no hair on their faces. Many of them were slavers, who often took creatures such as ourselves as prisoners and forced them to work. I had never seen one in the flesh, but now it looked as though many of them were heading straight towards us because, as the equines drew nearer, we could see that other, smaller creatures were perched on their backs.

'What shall we do?' I whispered.

'Let's not get excited,' said Papa. He was trying to sound calm, but I could sense the apprehension in

24

him. 'If we're lucky, they may not have seen us. Come on.'

And he led us quickly away, moving off at a sharp angle to the riders' approach. But we had only gone a little way, when we realised that the Uprights were changing their course to swing after us. It was only too clear that they had already seen us and were coming in pursuit.

'It's no use,' said Papa. 'We must run!'

Without further hesitation, we put our heads down and galloped away, just as fast as our hooves would carry us. Every so often, I risked a glance back over my shoulder and saw that the slavers were rapidly gaining on us. I could not run as quickly as my parents and I was uncomfortably aware that they were deliberately slowing their pace so as not to leave me behind.

'You must run faster!' bellowed Papa.

'I can't!' I shouted back at him.

I could hear the thunder of hooves behind me now and could smell the unfamiliar stench of the equines, a smell that was not like any wild creature that I had ever encountered, but one that spoke of misery and submission.

There were sounds too, the upright creatures calling to each other in a high keening tongue I could not understand. But the sound of it filled me with a nameless dread and I put everything I could into running, trying desperately to place some distance between my pursuers and me.

But they continued to gain on me, until I could sense them right on my heels, the noise of the galloping hooves drowning out all other sounds. My parents were by now frantic with worry, yelling at me to keep up with them, but my heart was beating so fast, I could hardly get my breath and I realised that I was never going to outrun these creatures, not if I ran to the very edge of the known world.

Just as I was thinking that, something long and snake-like came whizzing beneath me and wrapped itself around my front legs, which were suddenly jerked together with incredible force. I pitched forward, heels-over-head and hit the earth with a force that drove all the breath out of me. I rolled onto my back and tried to struggle upright, but then another of the snake things dropped around my neck and tightened so abruptly that it threatened to throttle the very life from me. I could feel an incredible force pulling at me, holding me in place and the next thing I knew, a couple of the Upright things had jumped down from their mounts and were pushing me to the ground, while they wrapped the snakes tighter around my legs so I could not move.

As I lay on my side, helpless, I saw Mama, in the same position as me, tied with the snakes and bawling my name out loud, as she struggled to get to me. I shouted back to her and one of the Uprights lashed a foot into my ribs, making me squeal with pain.

Then I heard a great bellow of anger and when I lifted my head, I saw Papa, charging back towards us, his mighty horns lowered to sweep any opposition out of his path. The Uprights that were holding me started shouting excitedly, but Papa kept on coming and I thought to myself: *he will chase them off, there's not a creature on the plains powerful enough to stand up to him!*

But just as I was thinking that, something inexplicable happened. A brightly plumed wooden stick seemed to spring out of Papa's shoulder and he roared in what sounded like pain. He kept on advancing though and then a second stick appeared from out of the side of his head and this time, he slowed in his tracks. I could see bright ribbons of blood oozing from the places where the sticks had appeared and then I saw a third stick, but this time, I realised that the thing was actually whizzing through the air and I saw it smack into Papa's chest with an impact that stopped him in his tracks.

I glanced back over my shoulder and saw that a couple of the Uprights were holding long curved wooden implements and they were using these to fling the plumed sticks through the air with great force. I saw that the sticks were topped with sharp stone barbs that glittered dangerously in the sunlight. I bellowed at them to stop what they were doing and their cruel faces looked down at me for an instant and then they laughed and carried on firing.

I looked back to Papa and two more sticks were jutting out from his throat and, as I watched, horrified, he sank slowly to his knees, gasping for breath. The blood was pumping down his shaggy hide and spraying from his nostrils and I saw a strange vacant stare come into his eyes. He made a last suffering moan and then he pitched over sideways and lay still.

'Papa!' I called, but he didn't respond.

I looked across to Mama, and she too was staring at his fallen body. She was making a pitiful sound, the sound a buffalope makes when it is sorrowful. My eyes filled with tears, because it seemed to me then that this was all my fault, that if we had stayed with the herd, perhaps everything would have been all right. My hollow words of the previous day rang in my ears.

We were trendsetters. We had really started something.

A couple of Uprights walked over to my father's body and they pulled bright metal talons from their belts. Then they leaned over him and . . .

28

I cannot speak of what happened next, not even after all this time. It was something that no young buffalope should ever have to witness and, to be sure, after the two Uprights started their grim work, I looked away and wept and I heard Mama weeping too. I cannot say how long I lay there but after a while, the snakes around my feet were loosened and I was pulled upright, the snake around my neck choking me, and I was pulled along behind an equine. I followed blindly because I no longer cared what happened to me. Papa was gone and I knew that I would never see his noble face again.

I managed to pull my head to the side for a moment, enough to glance back. What was left of him was lying on the plain and the sky was already dark with circling vultures. But then the Upright who held the other end of the snake gave it a vicious wrench and I was obliged to follow on.

'Mama!' I croaked. 'Mama! Are you alive?'

'Yes, little one,' she called back.

'What's going to happen to us?' I asked her.

'I don't know. Try to be brave. We have to-' But then she broke off with an exclamation of pain as something made a loud cracking sound.

'Mama!' I called. 'Mama, are you . . . ?' Then I found out what made the cracking sound, as something like a long vicious tongue lashed across my flanks, burning like fire; and after that, I was too scared to call out again.

I could only trot along behind my captors, as they led me across the plains to an uncertain future.

Chapter 4

In Captivity

For all of that day, I was dragged headlong through the dust, without pause or rest. Finally, when the sun was sinking towards the Western horizon, we came to some kind of a camp.

It was a poor and shabby looking place, a miserable collection of huts sitting to one side of a small stream. There were fires and I could smell the strange odour of burning meat, a smell I had only ever encountered once before, when a bolt of lightning had come down in the midst of the herd and killed several of my brothers and sisters. But the smell had stayed with me and it kindled fresh fears in my heart.

We came to a halt on the edge of the camp, and the Upright who had been leading me jumped down from his equine and tugged me the short distance to the stream, where he allowed me to slake my thirst.

Buffalope get most of the moisture they need from the grasses they eat, but I hadn't had a handful of food all day, so I drank greedily, gulping down mouthfuls of the cold, sweet water. Mama was brought to stand beside me and after we had both drunk our fill, we grabbed the opportunity to speak.

'Mama, what is this horrible place?'

'It must be the home of the Uprights, little one.'

'What do you think they want with us?'

'I don't know. Perhaps to make us work.'

'But, you saw what happened to Papa. And I can smell burning meat; you don't think .. ?'

'Hush child. Do not speak of what happened to Papa. He fought against the Uprights; and they killed him. Perhaps, if we do everything they want us to do, they will spare us.'

I was about to say something else, but then the Uprights that held us must have decided we'd had enough water; they jerked us viciously out of the stream and led us back through the village. There we were met by a chaos of shouts and yells, as more Uprights spilled out of the huts to get a better look at us.

There were yapping mutts that snapped at my hooves and clouds of choking smoke from the fires; every Upright in the place seemed to want to put his filthy paws on me. Some of them even forced open my jaws to look at my teeth and they were all shouting and laughing and slapping my rump. It was a relief when our captors pulled us on through the village and took us to some kind of enclosure made from logs just behind the huts, and flung us in there for the night.

Our first thought was escape and we moved along the four sides of the enclosure, looking for a way out, but the wooden barriers were high and stout and unnaturally straight and, even when we tried pushing against them, they didn't budge in the slightest. We quickly realised that we were trapped in here until somebody came to let us out.

'Don't waste your time,' said a voice in the gloom.

We looked up, startled, to discover that the words had issued from a skinny mule, who was standing in the very middle of the enclosure, watching us with interest. In the failing light, we hadn't even noticed him. I took an instant dislike to him, even though he was speaking the common language of the plains, one that is understood by every beast that dwells upon them.

He had a superior sneer and the air of one who thinks he knows better than anyone else. Unfortunately, he also had huge teeth that protruded beyond his lips and made everything he said sound like he was whistling a tune.

'Those logs are sunk deep into the ground; nothing is going to shift them.'

'Excuse me,' said Mama. 'We didn't realise there was somebody else in here.'

'That's quite understandable,' said the mule. 'You're bound to be somewhat confused. Just been caught, have you?'

'Yes, out on the plains,' said Mama. 'By the Uprights.'

'Neruvians,' said the mule. 'That's what they call themselves. Ne-ruv-i-ans.' He said it slowly, as though speaking to idiots. 'I've been here a while, I've picked up a few words of their tongue.'

'They killed my father!' I cried.

The mule nodded, and made a sort of tutting noise.

'I can't say I'm surprised,' he said. 'Probably put up some kind of resistance, did he?'

'I'm afraid so,' said Mama, hopelessly.

'Yes, well, you see, they don't waste time on creatures they don't think they can tame. That sort goes straight into the cooking pot.'

Mama gave a little gasp at this news, but the mule didn't even seem to notice.

'It's lucky for me that mules don't make good eating, otherwise that's where I'd be by now. But you buffalope . . .' He gave us a sly look. 'There's nothing these Neruvians like better than a bowl of buffalope stew.'

'Do you have to talk like that?' I asked him. 'Can't you see we're already upset?'

'I'm just being realistic,' said the mule. 'Sorry, I'm afraid I can sometimes be a bit blunt. My name's Jonah, by the way. And you two . . . ?'

'Bess,' said Mama, politely 'And this is my son.'

She told him my buffalope name, which is made by making a kind of snickering sound at the back of the throat. Of course, I didn't yet have the name that the Uprights put upon me: that came later.

'Well, I've been here for simply ages,' said Jonah. 'The Neruvians are animal traders; I've seen loads of creatures come and go. There were three equines in with me only a few days back, but they soon get snapped up. Everyone's in the market for a good equine these days.'

He snorted and shook his head to dispel a mantle of flies that were buzzing around him.

'None of the merchants that call here seem to want to buy an old mule,' he said. 'The Neruvians keep me for their children to play on and, believe you me, that's no picnic. The little blighters think nothing of hitting you with a length of stick to get you to gallop faster. My old flanks are riddled with scars, it's little wonder nobody wants to buy me.'

I felt like telling him that there might be other reasons

35

for that. He was quite the ugliest-looking creature I had ever seen. As well as the buck teeth, he also had floppy, fly-eaten ears and wiry grey hair that stood in unsightly tufts all over his body. He clearly had a tactless disposition to go with it, but I was already too upset to risk getting into a row with him, so I held my tongue.

'Would anyone wish to buy a pair of buffalope?' asked Mama.

Jonah snorted.

'It's unlikely the same person would buy the two of you,' he said. 'But buffalope are highly prized by merchants on account of they're so strong and they live to such a great age.'

He looked down at me.

'Not sure if anyone would want to take on a youngster like you,' he added. 'But you never know, it's a funny old world.'

'Will they give us anything to eat soon?' I asked hopefully.

'I'm afraid you've missed dinner,' said Jonah. 'But they should be round with a bit of mulch in the morning. It's not much to write home about, but it keeps the lupers from the gate, if you know what I mean.'

'Where did they catch you?' asked Mama.

I could tell that she was in no mood for conversation and was just trying to be polite, but Jonah seemed oblivious to her state.

'Oh, I was with my old master, crossing the plains. He was a potter and I used to carry the pots he made. We used to cross regularly from Torin to Jerebim. An arduous trip, mind, but my master could get four times the price for his work in Jerebim. He wasn't a bad sort, old Jeremiah. He fed me well enough and, though he worked me hard, he occasionally let me have the odd bit of a rest and you have to be grateful for small mercies in this life.'

'Whatever happened to him?' I asked.

'The Neruvians happened to him. They're a nasty bunch and no mistake. They murdered my poor master and took all of his pots and me along with them. Now what d'you think of that?'

'Murdered him?' gasped Mama. 'But . . . why? What had he done to them?'

'Nothing! They wanted the pots and the money they could make from them, simple as that. People like the Neruvians, they don't care who gets in their way. Villains, pure and simple.'

He glanced at Mama.

'As your husband has already discovered, to his cost,' he added. 'They'll doubtless be dining on him for weeks to come.'

Mama made a desperate little sound and turned away. She walked off a short distance, her head hanging low.

'Oops,' said Jonah. 'Sorry, didn't mean to speak out of turn. I was only saying . . .'

'Please don't say anything else,' I warned him.

I went to Mama, to try and comfort her.

'Ignore him,' I told her. 'He doesn't know what he's talking about.'

'I heard that!' said Jonah, but I took no notice.

'Mama,' I said. 'I feel terrible. If it hadn't been for me, we'd still be with the herd now, and Papa would still be . . .'

'You mustn't blame yourself,' she told me. 'If we'd stayed with the herd, all three of us might well be dead. Papa believed that going off on our own was the right thing to do and so did I. It was bad luck, nothing more. Come along, let's try to get some sleep.'

She led me over to one corner of the enclosure. We huddled down on the hard ground and snuggled into each other.

'Well, I'll say goodnight then, shall I?' said Jonah, sounding quite put out. 'Clearly you two are in no mood for conversation!'

I felt like telling him to shut up, but Mama raised her head and politely bid the old mule goodnight, so

I did the same. We didn't know how long we would have to share the enclosure with him and the last thing we needed was another enemy.

Exhausted as I was, I found it hard to go to sleep. And when I finally did, I was haunted by nightmares of Papa, charging towards me as the plumed sticks sprouted from his shaggy hide, one after the other . . .

Chapter 5

Sold!

The following morning, a long-haired, bare-chested Neruvian appeared at the enclosure and threw a bundle of mulch over the partition. By the time we had struggled upright and made our way across to it, the bulk of it had been chomped up by Jonah's massive teeth. Clearly he had been waiting for the arrival of the food and had neglected to warn us.

'Lovely morning,' he observed as we finished up the scraps he had left us, seemingly oblivious to the accusing looks we were giving him.

'Nothing like a bit of mulch to start off the day. Looks like it's going to be warm and sunny.'

Then he seemed to quail.

'Oh no,' he muttered.

I looked up and saw a bunch of ragged boys approaching the enclosure. A couple of them were carrying sticks. They unlatched a gate, let themselves in and made straight for Jonah, as if this was a regular pastime for them.

After a little while of watching their antics, I almost began to feel sorry for Jonah. They clambered up onto his back, two and three at a time and forced him to gallop round and round the enclosure, beating him mercilessly with the sticks if he failed to go fast enough. They pulled at his ears; they kicked his flanks; they hung onto his tail and made him drag them along – and all the while they laughed out loud at every grunt and squeal of protest he made.

At one point, a couple of the boys began to move towards us and Mama lowered her horns defensively, but then one of the adults in the village shouted something at the children and they turned back to Jonah and continued tormenting him. Presumably, we were deemed to be worth too much to use in such a sorry fashion.

After a while, the boys got bored and let themselves out again. Jonah stood there, his head bowed. I could see the fresh scars on his flanks, some of them dripping blood. We approached him carefully.

'Are you all right?' asked Mama.

He forced his goofy teeth into a grin.

'Oh, tolerable, tolerable,' he said, in a voice that was somehow much too jolly for his situation. 'Those little

41

devils like to play hard but, if you put your mind on something else, you can get through it. Hopefully, it will be the little girls next; they're a lot more respectful.'

And he limped away to a quiet corner of the paddock to be on his own for a while.

That first day, a few prospective buyers came to look us over, but nobody seemed interested. Jonah, of course, felt duty bound to keep up a running commentary on the proceedings.

'Now, this chappie here, he looks to me like a Keladonian. A lot of money in those parts. He's probably on the lookout for a noble equine to pull a fancy carriage. I shouldn't think a buffalope would be very high on *his* list! Ooh, now what about this lady? Hmm, she's got very strong arms and big hands, probably a washerwoman. You wouldn't want to be pulling a cartload of her stuff along, I can tell you!'

And so it went on, until the fourth day, when I saw a short little fellow wearing a bright yellow object on his head. He had a wizened, dark-skinned face and huge tufts of grey hair sprouting out from under his nose. He was studying Mama and me with evident interest.

'Aye, aye,' said Jonah, quietly, 'you two might have found yourselves a buyer. That fellow's a Berundian, you can tell by the turban . . .'

'The what?' I muttered.

'The yellow thing on his head! Berundians are famous for their oil and a big strong buffalope is just what they need to ... oh, hey up! Looks like something's happening!'

Sure enough, the Berundian was talking eagerly with one of the Neruvians, a big bare-chested fellow with strange patterns drawn on his shoulders and arms. The two men seemed to be talking intently for a moment, waving their hands and shaking their heads.

'Haggling over the price,' said Jonah, in his by now familiar know-all manner. 'Berundians are reputed to drive a hard bargain for whatever they buy. That's how come they're so prosperous. Watch for the handshake, that means they've made a deal.'

Right on cue, the two men spat onto their palms, clasped hands and shook each other's arms vigorously.

'Well, that's it,' said Jonah. 'Now we'll see which one of you it is.'

'Not both of us?' asked Mama hopefully.

'I very much doubt it, my dear. Most likely you; the little lad's a bit too small for heavy work.'

'It could be you,' Mama told him.

'Me? Oh, I don't think so. What would a Berundian want with an old mule?'

I glanced at him slyly.

43

'Perhaps he has lots of children,' I said.

'Oh, blimey, do you think so?' he muttered.

But now the Neruvian had taken a coil of the stuff that Jonah had told me the Uprights called 'rope' and he was letting himself into the enclosure. He came slowly towards us, fashioning the rope into a noose and the three of us stood there watching him apprehensively. He lifted a hand, twirled the rope a couple of times with well-practised ease and let it fly. It dropped around my neck and he began to drag me towards the gate.

'Mama!' I gasped.

She tried to make a move towards me, but the Neruvian was carrying the stinging thing that burned like fire and he lifted his arm and lashed Mama across her back, making her retreat. By the time she had recovered, the Neruvian had me out of the gate and was handing the rope to the Berundian.

Mama ran to the gate and called out to me and I began to bellow back, whereupon the Berundian raised a fist and punched me full on the snout, making my head spin. Then he pulled me over to a heavy wooden wagon pulled by a couple of equines and tied the end of the rope to the back of it. He climbed up onto the wagon, snapped the reins and the equines pulled away, dragging me behind them.

I tried resisting but I could not withstand the power of two full-grown equines and I had no option but to stumble along after the wagon, with Mama's lamenting cries ringing in my ears.

'Mama!' I called out.

The rope was so tight around my neck I could not even turn my head to look back at her.

'Mama, I'm frightened.'

'I will find you, little one!' she shouted after me. 'If it takes the rest of my days, I will find you.'

But it seemed hopeless. As I was pulled away into the vastness of the plains, I told myself that I would never see Mama again. Then the tears filled my eyes and I could no longer see where I was going.

Chapter 6

The Berundian Homestead

We must have travelled for three whole days before we came to the place that was to be my new home: a lonely farm, set in a deep and fertile valley some-where on the edge of the plains. As we crested a ridge, I could see it laid out below us. There was one large ramshackle house with smoke pouring from the chimney, some wooden cattle pens with various animals in them and, a short distance from that, a large orchard of drabnat trees, through which a wide stream flowed.

The Berundian slapped the reins and the equines descended a winding path until we were at the entrance to the farm. We went in and rode up to the front of the house. As we pulled to a halt, several Uprights came running out of the open door: a large, rather fat female wearing a strange white bonnet and a dress down to her feet, and two plump, yelling and rather excitable children, a boy and a girl.

They all came to the Berundian and started jabbering at him and he jabbered back; then the children noticed me, and the next thing I knew they were doing what the Neruvians had done, poking and prodding me, looking at my teeth, slapping my rump and laughing stupidly at my startled reactions. I was beginning to think that the Uprights were the stupidest and cruellest creatures in the known world and who could have blamed me?

After a while, the Berundian untied me from the wagon and led me across to one of the enclosures. In the very centre of it were two huge stone wheels lying flat and, connected to it by a long wooden pole and an intricate harness, was a huge buffalope, who was walking slowly round and round in a circle. As he walked, so the top wheel turned on the lower one with a low grinding sound.

'Papa?' I cried.

I don't know why I shouted that; I knew only too well that my father was dead and, sure enough, as the buffalope came around the circle, I saw his face and realised that this fellow was much older than Papa, his face and beard liberally peppered with grey. But

47

he had kind eyes and when he saw me, he gave me a friendly grunt and said, 'Hello, young sir, where did you spring from?'

The Berundian opened the gate of the enclosure, untied the rope from my neck and pushed me inside, closing the gate behind me. As I stepped in, to my amazement, the buffalope spoke to the Berundian, not in his own language, but in what sounded like the Upright tongue. The Berundian laughed and said something back and the two of them exchanged quite a few words before the Berundian nodded and walked away.

The buffalope looked at me, but he didn't stop walking around in a circle. I noticed now that an old Upright was tipping what looked like small green fruit into an opening at the top of the stones, while a second was filling containers with a clear yellow fluid, which flowed from an opening below the wheels.

'Welcome, young sir,' said the buffalope, in a deep, but gentle voice. 'I'm Brutus. The master would like the two of us to get to know each other.'

I looked at him.

'Brooo-tus? What kind of name is that?' I asked him.

'The name that my master has given me,' he said. 'Come, walk along with me; it's hard to talk to somebody you can't see most of the time.'

I must confess I didn't feel much like walking in circles, but I had questions that needed answers, so I fell into step with him.

'Now,' said Brutus. 'I presume you must have been captured from the wild?'

'Yes. From the great plains. My mother and I were captured by . . . Ner-uvi-ans, I believe they're called. My . . . my father was killed because he tried to fight them.'

Brutus nodded his head.

'It is not a good idea to fight back. Your father must have been brave to have attempted it.'

'He *was* brave,' I said. 'And wise. I miss him terribly.'

'What about your mother?' asked Brutus.

I could only shrug my shoulders.

'The last I saw of her, she was waiting to be sold.'

Brutus sighed.

'It's a hard world,' he said. 'And I know that right now you must think that my master is a barbarian.'

'I thought he was called a . . . Ber-und-ian.'

'Yes, that's what these people call themselves. A barbarian is something else, something fierce and terrible. But you will come to learn that my master is not so bad.'

'You speak the Upright tongue,' I said.

'Upright?' He laughed. 'That's a word I haven't heard

in a long time, a good old buffalope word. For your information, young sir, these creatures are called humans . . . unless of course, they are skinny little things with pointed ears, in which case they are known as elves.'

I tried the unfamiliar word.

'Hew . . . mans?' I said. 'Not . . . Berundians?'

'Well, they *are* Berundians, but that's just a type. They're called that because they come from Berundia, just as the Neruvians come from Neruvia and the Keladonians come from Keladon. But they're *all* humans. And I see you already know a few words of their language. See, it's not so hard is it?'

I frowned.

'What exactly are you doing?' I asked him.

'I'm grinding drabnat nuts,' he said, as though it were the most foolish question he had ever heard. He tossed his head towards the two great stone wheels. 'That stuff they are collecting is lamp oil. My master's oil is renowned throughout the land. It burns brighter, cleaner, longer. That's his slogan, by the way. I thought it up myself.'

I looked at him doubtfully and wondered why he would bother to help somebody who had enslaved him.

'Is this all you do?' I asked him. 'Walk round and round in circles?'

'It's an important job,' said Brutus, proudly. 'Repetitive, yes, but valuable, and I get good food and the occasional break, so it's not so very bad.'

I snorted.

'It doesn't look like my idea of fun,' I told him. 'In fact, I can't imagine a more boring existence.'

'Really?' He gave me a sly look. 'That's unfortunate,' he said.

'Why do you say that?'

'Because . . . well, Ebenezer hasn't actually said anything . . .'

'Ebe-nezer?' I prompted him.

'My master, the Berundian. He hasn't come out and told me, but I think I can guess his intentions. As you can see, I'm getting a little long in the beard. I won't be able to carry on doing this job for very much longer. So, he has obviously purchased you with a view to you becoming my replacement.'

I stared at him, horrified.

'You are jesting, I hope.'

He shook his great horned head.

'I seldom make jokes about such things,' he assured me. 'Oh, you are too small to turn these wheels as yet, but he probably wants to get as many years out of you as possible and that means he wants to start you just as soon as you are able.'

51

I must confess, the prospect of being chained to a wheel for the rest of my life was a nightmare.

'But ... I ... that's really not the kind of future I had in mind,' I protested.

Brutus shook his head.

'Nor I, for that matter. But you must understand, we buffalope do not get to choose our lives. We are but simple beasts of burden, here to serve humankind. We may not care for such a life but, if it is to be our lot, then we must embrace it and try to do our best.'

'You cannot always have thought that,' I argued. 'Did you not run wild upon the great plains, when you were younger?'

'Alas no, I have never known that life. My mother was working here when she bore me and it was she who taught me the way of the wheel. When she was taken away, I was ready to replace her ...'

'Taken away?' I didn't much like the sound of this. 'Taken where?'

Brutus shrugged his massive shoulders.

'I do not know. One morning she was complaining to me that she had gone lame in one foot. That night the master took her away and I never saw her again. I believe he said something about a rest home.'

'Oh yes?' I said. Even at my tender age, I was shocked by his naivety.

'Yes, she went to the rest home and I took her place at the wheel.'

My mind began to work furiously. I thought about the brutal fate that had been handed out to Papa, and I thought about Ebenezer's fat wife and his plump children and I imagined that in their home there must be a big cooking pot. It didn't take a mastermind to work out where Brutus's mother must have gone, or, for that matter, where Brutus would be bound once I was ready to take his place. But clearly the idea had never occurred to him and somehow I could not bring myself to voice my suspicions.

So we continued to walk around in circles all the rest of that day, until the sun went down, which is when the Berundian's two workmen unhitched Brutus from the wheel and led the two of us to a strange wooden building, where we were given mulch to eat and settled down for the night. But I noticed that, when the workmen left, they secured the heavy doors, making it clear that there was no escape. No matter how Brutus liked to dress it up, we were prisoners.

That night I slept only fitfully, haunted by the thought of poor Mama and what might be happening to her. I dreaded to think of her being sold to humans who would treat her cruelly but, even more, I dreaded the thought of her *not* being sold and ending up in the

Neruvian's cooking pot. When I did sleep, it seemed only for a few moments. I woke to the sound of a cock crowing and Brutus cheerfully telling me it was time to start work again. Then it was back to the enclosure and the wheel, endlessly turning round and round.

Chapter 7

Brutus

Please don't get me wrong. Brutus was one of the nicest creatures I ever had the good fortune to meet. He was polite and jovial and it was he who started me on the long process of learning the human tongue. But the thing is, he was incredibly thick.

He couldn't see that he was being exploited and it was pointless to try and tell him that his master was a cynical swine who would use him until he was fit to drop – and would then chuck him in the nearest cooking pot without so much as turning a hair. He saw himself as a partner in his master's business but, I ask you, what kind of a partner is it who never enjoys one privilege and who ends up being eaten by the very people whom he has worked so hard for?

The language thing started when Brutus suggested to me that I might surprise the workmen one morning by bidding them 'Good morning!' in their own language. I learned it in a moment and asked him to teach me some more. That was when I realised I had a natural aptitude for speaking the human tongue. Mind you, compared to the complexities of buffalope, it's dead simple.

Brutus himself could speak a fair few phrases, but wasn't exactly what you would call a great conversationalist. Once I had learned the extent of what he could teach me – which took but a few weeks - I found myself eager to learn more, which I did by getting on speaking terms with the two workmen, who were called Harold and James. I would ask them one of my simple questions and would listen intently to their replies, memorising as much as I could; but to be honest, they weren't exactly what you'd call intellectuals. Their conversations ran to the state of the weather and the price of a flagon of ale.

I don't know why I had such an urge to learn the language of a race of creatures that had done me so much harm. Perhaps I wanted to prove that I was as clever, if not more so, than they were. And perhaps I had realised that, if I didn't want to end up in a menial position like Brutus, I would need to be able to deal with the humans on their own terms and the best way to do that would be to speak to them.

All the while this was going on, I was keeping an eye out for a possible way of escape. For the time being at least, I wasn't ready to replace Brutus, but I was painfully aware that I was growing bigger day by day and it wouldn't be too long before his harness would make a proper fit around my shoulders.

The thing is: if I did manage to escape, where would I go? This part of the world was unfamiliar to me and it was a long way back to the great plains. And, even if I did manage to make it there, what hope was there for a young buffalope on his own? So many questions and not a suitable answer for one of them.

And then, one day, something happened that once again would change my life. It is from the smallest things that the biggest changes can occur.

Brutus hurt his leg. It happened like this.

There we were, the two of us, going round and round in our endless circles, me practising my human talk, Brutus providing a few answers, when, unexpectedly, a piece of drabnat fruit fell from the loader and rolled into his path. As I'm sure you know, drabnats are very hard, round objects and one of Brutus's front hooves came down on it, making him skid and splaying his front leg out in front of him at an awkward angle. I heard the crack of a bone and Brutus gave a grunt of pain. He struggled back to his usual stance, but when he tried to walk forward, he found he couldn't put any weight on the injured leg.

Harold and James came forward and asked him what he thought he was playing at.

'Brutus hurt leg,' he said. 'Think ankle twisted.'

'What?' cried Harold. 'That's no use! You'll have to go on. We've a big order of lamp oil to supply; the master will be furious.'

'I cannot help,' said Brutus calmly. 'Cannot put weight on leg.'

Harold and James had a muttered conversation and then James hurried off to fetch the master. After a short while, Ebenezer came striding out of the house, an expression on his face that suggested that somebody was holding a piece of dung under his nose. I saw to my concern that he was carrying the stinging thing, that Brutus had told me was called a whip.

'What's the meaning of this nonsense?' growled Ebenezer. 'Why have you stopped work?'

'Master,' began Brutus. 'I hurt leg.'

'Don't be ridiculous, a great big beast like you; get moving at once!'

'But Master, I . . .'

'At once, I say.'

Ebenezer lifted the whip and lashed poor Brutus across the flanks. He tried pitifully to hobble along for a few steps, but had to give up with a gasp of pain.

'It's no good, Master, I . . .'

He broke off as once again, the whip licked across his back. I stood and watched in mute disgust as Ebenezer continued to beat his good and faithful servant.

'Leave Brutus alone!' I shouted, in my halting way. 'He injured, need rest.'

Ebenezer paused to look at me. I don't think he had heard me speak human before. His eyes narrowed and a sly look came into them.

'If you don't keep a civil tongue in your head, I'll give you a taste of the whip too,' he said.

'That not help get things done! You want drabnat oil, you let Brutus rest.'

Ebenezer's face flushed red.

'If he needs to rest so badly, perhaps you'd like to take his place?' he growled.

'Oh no, Master,' protested Brutus. 'Lad not strong enough turn wheel. It cripple him.'

'And I will be crippled . . . financially crippled, if I do not supply this order in time,' snapped Ebenezer.

'Perhaps I have little time off?' suggested Brutus. 'I been good worker before today, Master. If I rest a while . . . I be better soon.'

Ebenezer began to pace up and down, as though deliberating what to do. Finally, he seemed to come to a decision.

'Very well," he said. 'I'll give you the rest of the day and tonight. Tomorrow morning, first thing, you go back on the wheel. And if you can't do it, then he shall go in your place . . .'

He pointed a finger at me.

'. . . whether he's up to it or not. And as for you . . .'

He pointed at Brutus.

'If he takes your place, you'll go where your mother went before you.'

'My mother?' Brutus looked at Ebenezer with interest. 'Oh, rest home!' He nodded, seemed to accept this news.

But I wasn't about to accept it.

'Where is rest home?' I asked.

'Ebenezer glared at me.

'Keep your snout out of this!' he said.

'He only ask,' said Brutus. He thought for a moment. 'I would like to know, too.'

Ebenezer looked as though he might be about to say something, but he must have thought better of it.

'You'll find out,' he said, his voice laden with threat, 'if you're not fully up to scratch tomorrow morning.'

He gestured to Harold and James.

'Put them in the barn for the night and give them something to eat.'

And, with that, he stalked away.

We were led to the barn, poor Brutus limping every step of the way. Once inside, he settled himself carefully onto the hay with a groan of pain.

'Who'd have thought that a little thing like a drabnat could cause so much trouble?' he said, talking more fluently in his own tongue. 'Still, at least we have this afternoon off, so it's not all bad news, is it?'

I was trying to come to terms with my own bad news: the thought that tomorrow I would be strapped to those great stone wheels and made to turn them. Once I was in that harness, I thought, there would be no hope for me. I would live and die in them.

'Do you honestly think your leg's going to be better by tomorrow?' I demanded.

'Who can say?' murmured Brutus. 'It certainly doesn't feel like something that could heal overnight. The leg is very swollen.'

'Which means that I shall be tied to that wheel in your place, and you . . . you'll be . . . where your mother went,' I said.

'Yes, that was interesting, don't you think? He's certainly never mentioned the idea of me going there before. Where do you suppose the rest home is? I like to think it's a nice green paddock with perhaps a few other old buffalope to pass the time of day with.'

I stared at him. Like I said, thick.

'Brutus, haven't you worked it out yet?' I cried. 'Where do you *think* your mother went?'

'Well . . . to the rest home. You heard Ebenezer, she was taken to . . .'

'Oh for goodness sake, wake up and smell the clover! Your poor mother didn't go to any rest home, she went into the bellies of your master and his family!'

'Into—?'

He broke off and stared at me open-mouthed.

'What do you mean, into their bellies? How could . . . ?'

'They *ate* her, Brutus. And they'll eat you if you can't work that wheel tomorrow. . . without a moment's hesitation.'

He laughed then, but it wasn't very convincing.

'That's . . . ridiculous,' he said. 'My master wouldn't . . . he wouldn't do something like that. The very idea!' He tossed his head dismissively. 'You're just a youngster, what do you know?'

'Enough to tell when somebody can't be trusted,' I said. 'And I wouldn't trust Ebenezer any further than I could butt him.'

'He . . . he wouldn't lie to me. We've been together for years.'

'Well, why don't you ask him?' I said. 'Tomorrow morning, when he comes for you. Why not see what he has to say about it?'

Brutus snorted.

'I will,' he said. 'Don't you worry!'

He put his great head down onto the straw and lay there brooding over the matter, while I ate my hay in silence. After a while he said, in a smaller voice than before.

'Do you . . . do you *really* think that's what happened?'

'Of course it is,' I told him. 'I didn't want to be the one to tell you. But you see, Brutus, your master is not the fair and honest creature you'd like to think he is. He's like the rest of his kind, out for what he can get. And the likes of you and me, we're just possessions, to be used or discarded as he pleases.'

Brutus sighed.

'I do hope you're wrong,' he said. 'I've often talked to him about my mother . . . speculating on where the rest home might be . . . but he's never really given me a straight answer.'

'Well,' I said, 'he's hardly likely to tell you he ate her with a nice bowl of gravy, is he? That wouldn't have been much of an incentive to keep you working at the wheel.'

I know it was a terrible thing to say. But Brutus had to learn the awful truth somehow. Besides, it had occurred to me that tomorrow morning would be make or break time for me. I kept thinking about those heavy stone wheels, turning round and round, and I pictured myself shackled to them, performing the same meaningless task for the rest of my days.

One thing was certain. I knew that I could not let it happen. I'd die first.

Chapter 8

Make or Break

They came for us at cockcrow. The doors were unlatched and Ebenezer strutted in, carrying his whip, with Harold and James walking just behind him. He gave Brutus an unsympathetic look.

'Well?' he demanded. 'How's the leg?'

'Better, I think,' said Brutus, carefully raising himself up onto his feet.

But I could see the pained expression on his face as he did so. His leg wasn't healed at all.

'Then you're ready to start work again?' asked Ebenezer.

'Soon,' said Brutus, calmly. 'First, need to speak about mother.'

'Your mother?' Ebenezer's eyes narrowed suspiciously. 'What about her?'

Brutus edged a little closer.

'You recall, Master, when you first take her away, you say you take her to rest home?'

'Er . . . yes,' said Ebenezer, warily. 'What of it?'

'Master please be good enough to tell Brutus where this place is.'

I noticed that Harold and James had to suppress smiles when Brutus asked this. Ebenezer just shrugged his narrow shoulders.

'I forget exactly,' he said. 'Somewhere off towards . . .'

He waved a hand in dismissal. 'Come along, we need to get on with the oil. I have important people waiting for this order.'

But Brutus shook his head.

'No work till you answer question,' he said.

His voice was still calm but his intent was evident.

'Oh er . . . it was somewhere near Torin, I believe,' said Ebenezer. 'Yes, I forget the exact details; it was years ago.'

'And . . . she is still alive?'

'Who cares?' snarled Ebenezer. 'Listen, I've had about enough of this nonsense. Move your flea-bitten carcass out of there and . . .'

'My young friend here say she never go to rest home. He say she go into your cooking pot.'

There was a silence, so deep you could have heard

a piece of straw turning over. Ebenezer stared at Brutus and the guilt was written all over his face. After a few moments, he found his tongue and tried to protest.

'What . . . nonsense!' he cried. 'The very idea! And why you would listen to a mere calf, is beyond me. Now look, I'm through being polite here.'

He raised the whip threateningly.

'If you don't make a move, I swear I'll beat you until you beg for mercy.'

But Brutus was nodding his great horned head.

'He was right,' he said. 'Brutus has been blind all these years. There is no rest home. You eat my mother and you eat me, if I not get well. I who work for you, year after year, never complain. You would put me on plate to feed family.'

Ebenezer lost his temper then.

'Yes, of course I would!' he yelled. 'Who d'you think you are? You're just a beast of burden with ideas above your station. I own your miserable hide, I paid good money for it and I'll use it as I see fit. And if that means an extra meal for my family, so be it! Now shut your stupid mouth and get moving!'

He raised the whip and lashed it across Brutus's huge back, but the buffalope barely flinched. He put down his head and pawed the ground with his injured front leg. Then he glanced briefly at me.

'You get away from here, lad,' he murmured. 'Don't make the mistake I did.'

The whip cracked across his back a second time and he lifted his head, to stare at Ebenezer with cold intent. He gave a great rumbling bellow of anger. Then he charged.

It all happened very quickly. One moment Ebenezer was standing there, framed in the open doorway. The next, there was a terrible impact as Brutus's great horns hit him in the chest and lifted him clean off his feet. Harold and James scattered frantically out of the way as Ebenezer was carried out of the barn, yelling in terror.

I took the opportunity to scramble upright and I made a run for the doorway. James, realising my intention, made a leap for me, trying to throw his arms around my neck, but I swung my head to meet him and my horns caught him in the face with a dull thud. I flung him aside like a sack of rubbish.

Then I was out of the barn and running in Brutus's wake and I could see that the big buffalope was still carrying Ebenezer towards his house and he wasn't slowing his pace at all, even though he must have been in agony on his injured leg. As I watched in amazement, Brutus slammed Ebenezer against the door of his house, which flew off its hinges and then they disappeared inside and there was a great crashing sound from within, mingled with the terrified screams of Ebenezer's wife and children.

I raced around the side of the house, heading for the plains beyond and, as I ran past the back of the building, I heard another crash and when I looked back over my shoulder, I saw Ebenezer's broken and bloodied body flying through the back window amidst a blizzard of broken glass. He hit the ground, rolled over several times and did not move.

I didn't slow my pace at all but just kept going, bounding up the twisting track that led from the farm and galloping over the ridge beyond. I had only a vague notion of my direction, but I believed that I was heading for the great plains and I wasn't going to let anything stop me.

I ran and ran until I thought my lungs would burst and, only when I was totally exhausted, did I slow to a canter, a trot, and then a walk. I looked back the way I had come and I could not see anybody following me. I was free once more, but totally alone in the vastness of an unfamiliar landscape.

There was nothing for it but to start walking.

Chapter 9

Wandering

I walked for days and nights, not wanting to stop until I found some familiar territory. But everything here looked strange to me. I had lost my sense of direction and could not seem to find a path.

At last, I crested a ridge and found myself looking down at a comforting flatness that resembled the great plains from which I had been dragged; but where that land would have been rich with lush grass, here it was arid, red soil with just the occasional tuft of scrub poking through the earth.

I told myself that I must be a lot further South than my home ground and that I needed to turn North, if I wanted to get back to it. Except that, mixed up as I was, I was no longer really sure which way *was* North. I would have to wait for the sunrise and try to work out my position from that. Meanwhile, I descended the ridge and kept moving, telling myself that I was lucky to be away from Ebenezer's clutches and the awful fate that he had in store for me.

That night, I huddled down on the ground, jerking rudely awake at every sound that came out of the night, a mixture of hoots and howls and chirruping that set my poor nerves on edge. It's little wonder that I've suffered with my nerves all my life, after the trials I suffered in that remote spot.

At dawn the next morning, I got myself upright and went on my way again, keeping the sun on my left side and hoping against hope that I was heading in the right direction. I wished that Mama and Papa were here to guide me, but Papa was gone and I seriously doubted that I would ever see Mama again.

It was that afternoon when I realised that I was being followed. I'd chanced to look over my shoulder and I saw several small creatures trailing me at a distance. I snorted and turned to have a proper look, then realised with a jolt of horror that it was a pack of wild mutts, small, grey spindly creatures with hideous spotted backs, ugly black snouts and thick, bushy tails. I did a quick headcount and there were seven of them.

I had seen enough mutts following the great herd to know how these creatures operated. They would follow us for miles and they never gave up, not until

71

they got some poor straggler on his own, and then it took the combined horns of the adult males to drive them away. But here I was, totally alone. Who was going to help me?

I turned and began to run and the mutts barked and howled and took off after me, running easily on their big wide-splayed paws, their tongues lolling. Ahead of me there was nothing but more dry plains, stretching as far as the eye could see. I began to think that I was doomed. Just my luck, I thought, to escape from that rotten Berundian, only to land myself in even deeper trouble. It was enough to make me want to spit.

I ran for mile after mile until my heart felt like it was going to burst, but I could not shake the mutts off my trail. Finally, near to exhaustion, I turned and lowered my horns. The mutts closed around me, staying low on their bellies and circling, as they looked for an opening.

The first of them dashed at my rear hooves and I launched a wild kick that caught her in the chest and sent her spinning. But, immediately, her brothers and sisters were upon me in six different places, snapping at my legs, my flanks, my tail. One of them got his powerful teeth into one of my haunches and I bellowed with pain and swung around, lifting him clear off his feet.

Another made a leap for my throat, but I swung my head hard to the side and one of my horns caught her a crack across the skull. She yelped and went rolling away across the ground.

A desperate struggle followed. I felt pain from every quarter as a succession of teeth locked into my flesh, but I kicked and bucked and stamped and swung my horns and sometimes I felt the snapping of bones beneath my hooves and, I have to tell you, it felt pretty good. But it was a fight I could not hope to win. My strength was near to failing me and I must have been bleeding from a dozen places, yet I would not capitulate and I kept on fighting with every bit of strength left in my body.

Finally, I stood on my failing legs and saw that there were just three of the mutts left standing, their brothers and sisters either dead or crippled. One brute, bigger than his companions, advanced slowly towards me. There was a look of sheer malignance in his yellow eyes and, as he came forward, I could see the saliva dripping from his jaws. I knew that he was about to leap at my throat and that I needed to repel his attack, but I no longer had the strength to swat him away. I lowered my head and waited for the deathblow.

Instead, I heard a sudden yelp of pain. I looked up and saw the three mutts running away in apparent terror. The biggest of them had a plumed stick in his side, the kind of thing that had killed Papa. For an instant, I felt exhilarated. I was alive! But my delight was short-lived as it occurred to me that it must be the Neruvians, come to claim back their property.

I swung giddily around to look behind me. I saw a strange carriage on wheels that was hitched to a single equine. The side of the carriage was gaily decorated with colours and strange squiggly lines. I was too young and inexperienced to recognise these as human words. Beside the carriage stood a man, holding a bow. He was dressed like no other human I had ever seen. His clothes were covered in brightly coloured stripes and he wore a strange kind of hat, a comical looking thing that ended in three prongs, each with a small jingling bell.

I stood there looking at the human through bleary eyes as he walked slowly towards me. My first impulse was to charge at him, to try and escape, but the man was smiling at me and there was a kindness in his eyes that I had seen in no other human.

'Hello,' he said. 'You're in a terrible state, aren't you? It's lucky that I happened along.'

I opened my mouth to ask him who he was and what he wanted, but all that emerged was a long moan of pain.

'Here, you look ready to drop,' he said.

He put a hand onto my neck and grabbed a hank of hair.

'Better get you into my caravan,' he said. 'Young as you are, I won't be able to carry you if you fall down here.'

He led me to the back of the thing he had called a 'caravan'. There were steps leading up into it, but he pulled out a long flat piece of wood from within and made a ramp up which he pushed and prodded me. I was too weak to resist. I found myself standing in a strange little place full of weird and wonderful-looking objects, the like of which I had never seen before.

Then my legs gave out and I slumped down onto the wooden floor with a long sigh. I was dimly aware of the human pushing the plank of wood in beside me.

'Get some rest,' he said. 'We haven't far to go.'

After a short silence, the floor beneath me began to rock and shudder, as though we were moving.

I craned my head around trying to get a better look at the wonders around me, but I was tired, so very tired. My heavy eyelids came down and I slept like the dead.

Chapter 10

Alexander

His name was Alexander Darke and, when I met him, he was a young and, it must be said, fairly unsuccessful jester. I didn't know that straight away, of course. I didn't even know what a jester was. All that came later, when I had recovered my strength.

To begin with, I was very ill and the memories I have of that time are of lying on a pile of straw in a warm, dry stall, being tended by the man in the strange striped clothing and his young wife, who had the petite stature and pointed ears of the elf-creatures that old Jonah had once described to me.

They washed the blood from me and tended my wounds; they poured water down my throat and spoke gentle words, which were a revelation after everything I had suffered at the hands of other Uprights; they didn't seem to want anything of me other than my survival.

After a few days of their tender ministrations, I finally felt strong enough to speak.

'Thank you,' I said, as the man leaned over me, inspecting the poultice on one of the wounds in my side.

He rocked back a little, his expression one of surprise.

'You can speak!' he said.

Bit of an obvious remark, under the circumstances, but I refrained from commenting on it.

'Sarah, come over here! The buffalope can speak. He just said thank you!'

The elvish woman came over to kneel beside me. She looked at me with interest and I noted how pretty she was, with her dark curling hair and her jet black eyes.

'Are you sure?' she asked him. 'Perhaps it just *sounded* like hello.'

'No really, he looked up at me and . . .'

'He speaks true,' I told her. 'I know words of human tongue. My friend Brutus teach me.'

The two of them laughed delightedly.

'This Brutus has taught you very well,' said the man. 'I must say it's good to see that you're on the mend. When I first came across you, I wouldn't have given a croat for your chances. Those mutts had worked you over something terrible.'

'I is in your debt, sir.'

'Oh, no need to be so formal! I am Alexander Darke. And this is my lovely wife, Sarah.'

I nodded. 'And I am called—'

And I said my buffalope name, making the snickering sound at the back of my throat. The two of them looked at each other.

'I doubt that we'll be able to pronounce that,' said Alexander. 'Would you object if we gave you a human name, something we could say more easily?'

'I not mind,' I assured them.

'Then we shall call you . . .'

Alexander thought for a moment.

'Max,' he said. 'What d'you think, Sarah? He looks like a Max to me.'

'I think it suits him. But what does Mr Buffalope think of it?'

'Max,' I said.

I rather liked the sound of it. It seemed strong and dependable, qualities that I like to think I have in abundance.

'I very happy to have this name,' I said.

'That's settled then,' said Alexander. 'Now, Max, I'm no doctor, but I'd say the elvish poultices that Sarah made for your wounds are weaving their magic. You'll be healed in no time.'

He studied me thoughtfully.

'Where were you going when I found you?' he asked. 'You became separated from your herd, perhaps?'

I shook my head and winced at the pain this caused.

'I left herd days back,' I said. 'There was sickness. Then I caught by evil Neruvians who sell me to cruel master. He chain me and want to make me grind drabnat fruit. I was fleeing from him when mutts attack.'

Sarah frowned.

'I don't blame you for running away,' she said. 'It sounds like an awful life. But you are only a youngster. What of your parents?'

I sighed.

'Papa dead; shot with feather-sticks by bad men. Mama they take, too. I not know where she be.'

Sarah's pretty face registered sadness.

'You poor thing,' she said.

She reached out a hand to stroke my head. Then she glanced at Alexander Darke, as though asking him an unspoken question, and he nodded, as though he understood perfectly.

'Well, listen, Max,' she said, 'you can stay here as long as you wish. Once you are stronger, we have a nice big paddock with plenty of grass. You'll be good company for Betty.'

'Bett-ee?' I murmured.

'Our equine. She has a friendly disposition, I should think the two of you will get along fine.'

'I can work,' I said. 'To earn my keep.'

Alexander waved a hand dismissively.

'Oh, don't worry about that. We'll see how it goes when you're properly healed. For the time being, just think about getting better.'

'Thank you,' I said again. 'Your skins . . . I never see skins like these before.'

'Skins?'

He looked puzzled, then glanced down at himself.

'Oh, you mean my *clothes*! This is a jester's outfit. That's my trade.' He glanced at Sarah. 'At least, I hope it will be. It's early days yet.'

I gazed up at him from my place on the straw.

'Please . . . what is this . . . jayster?'

Alexander grinned self-consciously.

'I suppose it wouldn't mean very much to a buffa-lope,' he agreed. 'A jester is a man who makes a fool of himself for a living. You know, tells jokes, prances about, falls over . . . that kind of thing.'

'I have seen humans like this,' I admitted. 'But I not know they get *paid* for it.'

Alexander laughed out loud.

'That's very good!' he said. 'If you don't mind, I might borrow that.'

'You are welcome,' I said, not really understanding what he meant.

'Of course, I'm not really getting paid all that much at the moment,' said Alexander, 'because I'm just starting out. But I hope, in time, that I will become famous, like Jonathan Jolly.'

'Jon-ath-on Joelie?' I echoed. 'Who is this?'

'You've not heard of him? Oh, he's famous! The master of mirth, the king of comics, the lord of laughter! He's absolutely rolling in it!'

'Rolling in what?' I asked. 'Mud?'

'No! In money. Why, it's said that the Royal Court of Jerebim pay him three gold crowns for every appearance.'

'Money isn't everything,' Sarah told him. 'And I think you're every bit as funny as Jonathan Jolly. Funnier, in fact. But he's been around forever. It takes time to build a reputation'

'Not too long, I hope,' said Alexander. 'We've debts mounting up and tradesmen won't wait forever to be paid.'

'You'll get there,' Sarah assured him. And she leaned over and gave him a peck on the cheek.

I have to tell you, it did my heart good to see a young couple so much in love with each other. I told myself I had been very lucky to find two Uprights as kind and giving as the Darkes. And, from that very moment, I began to get better.

Chapter 11

A Brand New Start

In just a few days Alexander was able to get me back onto my feet and he led me out into the paddock he had spoken of, which, as he had promised, was full of sweet green grass. Which was lucky, because, I don't mind telling you, I was *starving*. And in the paddock, I found Betty waiting for me.

She was a nice old girl, there's no two ways about it. As soon as I arrived, she was there, using the common language of the plains to enquire after my health and saying how worried she'd been when she'd first laid eyes on me. When she found out what had happened to my parents, tears came into her lovely brown eyes and I think from that moment she saw herself as my foster mother, always looking out for me and even offering me a warm flank to snuggle against when the nights were cold.

She told me that she had worked for Alexander for many years and his father before him. She said that Alexander was quite the nicest master an equine could hope to have and that he had never so much as raised his voice to her, let alone a whip. When I told her about Ebenezer and poor Brutus, she was quite disgusted.

'I'm afraid there are many humans like that,' she admitted. 'We should be thankful that we have ended up with two of the best of them.'

'So, what's this jester stuff all about?' I enquired as I munched a mouthful of grass. 'Alexander did try to explain it to me, but I didn't really follow what he was saying.'

Betty snorted.

'It is very odd,' she said. 'As I understand it, the humans like to have a good laugh. So much so, that they are willing to pay money for it. You ... understand what money is, I suppose?'

'Yes, the little round shiny things? My old master, Ebenezer, was very fond of that stuff.'

She nodded.

'So, my master puts on his costume and he travels to a place where there are lots of humans ... say a tavern or a town square. And he gets up in front of them and, er ... he talks to them.'

I looked at her.

'That's it?' I said. 'He *talks* to them?'

'Well yes, and he falls about a bit and looks stupid, but mostly he just talks, and what he says must be pretty funny, because people start to laugh and, when he's finished talking, he goes around with his jester's hat and some of the people throw coins into it.'

'What does he talk about, exactly?'

Betty sighed.

'I don't really know. I've never mastered the human tongue. I can understand the odd word, but that's all.'

She thought for a moment.

'I think he talks about people in the town and says things to make them look silly.'

'And they pay him for that?' I shook my head. 'Takes all kinds, I suppose.'

Those early days with the Darke family were among the happiest and most leisurely of my life. There wasn't much to do but eat the grass in the paddock and grow in size and strength, which I did very effectively. Every morning, Alexander would come out to harness Betty to the wagon, in order to travel to his next performance and this was my opportunity to engage my master in conversation, something which he seemed to enjoy. He never failed to be delighted by the fact that he had a buffalope that could talk; and he encouraged me to learn more and more of the human tongue.

The months passed and winter came. Betty and I were moved into the nice snug stables and were given bundles of hay to eat. Alexander and Sarah often spent hours talking to me, while the cold winds raged outside and Betty snoozed in the stall next to me.

By this time, I had pretty much reached my adult size and was speaking fluent human. I understood a lot more about Alexander's line of work by now and he had fallen into the habit of trying out his new material on me. He always maintained that if he could get *me* to laugh, then he could get anyone to do so. I don't like to boast, but, even in those early days, I was helping him to refine and develop the material that, in due course, would make him the Prince Of Fools, one of the most celebrated jesters in the land.

'Right, Max,' he would say, 'see what you think of this lot.'

And he would begin . . .

'Did you hear about the brigand who insisted on taking a bath every time he committed a robbery?'

'No Master; why did he do that?'

'So he could make a clean getaway!'

(A dreadful joke, I know, but Alexander had a way of telling the most unpromising jokes and making them funny. It was something to do with his voice and his expression and the insane grin on his face as he told it.)

'Two lupers are eating a jester. One says to the other, "Does this taste *funny* to you?"'

'Ah yes, not bad!'

I liked to give him the odd bit of encouragement; it seemed to spur him on.

'A man goes to see a doctor, complaining that he feels terrible. The doctor examines him and says that he's got a fatal illness. The man is horrified. "How long have I got?" he asks. "You've got ten," says the doctor. "Ten?" cries the man. "Do you mean ten months, ten weeks, ten days . . . what?" The doctor ignores him and carries on talking, "nine – eight – seven . . ."'

'Oh, I see! Very comical!'

'Here's another one. Why is six afraid of seven?'

'I don't know, Master.'

'Because seven ate nine!'

And so it went on. These were wonderful days. I was a young bull in my prime, I had chanced upon two of the nicest humans you could ever hope to meet, I had no responsibilities and I could see no reason why the situation should ever change. The trials and tribulations of my early days seemed far away and, for the most part, I was content with my life.

But, if I have learned one thing in my many years, it is simply this. Nothing stays the same for very long.

It is the changes in our lives that make us what we are and, once again, things were about to happen that would send me in a different direction.

Chapter 12

Partners

It happened the following spring. Betty and I had been out of the barn and in the paddock for several weeks and I began to notice that she wasn't quite her usual self. She would come back from one of Alexander's appearances and she'd be quite out of breath; no sooner had she eaten a mouthful of her evening meal, than she'd be off in her favourite corner, fast asleep and snoring.

I noticed too that, whereas she used to be up at first light, waiting eagerly for Alexander's approach, now she tended to sleep on until he was at the gate, calling her.

One evening, after feeding us both, Alexander hung around, chatting to me about this and that, seemingly in no hurry to go into the house. He waited until Betty was asleep and then he starting talking with more purpose.

'Have you noticed any difference in Betty, lately?' he asked.

I nodded.

'She seems to be tired all the time,' I said. 'It's a shame, because I really used to look forward to our conversations in the evening and now I never seem to exchange more than a few words with her.'

'She's not getting any younger,' he said.

I gave him a questioning look. Humans have a tendency to say stupid things, from time to time. Of course she wasn't getting younger, none of us were, but I let the comment pass. What he was really saying was that Betty was getting *old* and I couldn't really argue the point.

'I'm beginning to think that it might be time to let her have a good rest,' continued Alexander.

An alarming thought flashed across my mind. I thought of Brutus's mother, and the 'rest home' she had been sent to; but then I looked at Alexander and knew that he would not dream of pulling such a cruel trick on Betty. With Alexander Darke – at least in those days – cruelty was something he hadn't the first idea about.

'Indeed, Master, I'd say she deserves one,' I said.

He frowned.

'I've told you before, you don't have to call me that. Alexander will do just as well.'

'It pleases me to call you Master,' I assured him. 'Rest assured, if I did not wish to call you that, nothing would ever get me to say it . . . even if you were to stick lighted tinder sticks into my hooves.'

'I'm sure it won't come to that,' he said. 'But, about Betty . . .'

'Well, as I was saying. She has earned herself a rest, of that I'm sure. I know she has worked hard for you for many years . . . and your father before you.'

Alexander nodded.

'Problem is,' he said, 'who could I find to take her place? It would have to be somebody strong, dependable . . . and fearless.'

'Fearless?' I murmured.

'Oh yes, sometimes I have to travel through lawless territory to get to a performance. There are encounters with brigands, conmen, wild beasts . . . all kinds of peril. But you know, creatures as reliable as Betty are very hard to find.'

I gazed at him for a moment, wondering why he wouldn't just come out and ask me.

'Well, Master,' I said. 'In the absence of any alternatives, I wonder if you would consider me?'

'You?'

He looked at me, as though the idea hadn't even occurred to him.

'Oh, but Max, I couldn't ask you to haul that heavy caravan.'

'Why ever not?' I asked him. 'I'm fully grown now, and stronger than Betty ever was. I could pull that thing for miles without turning a hair.'

'Yes, but . . . well, you have already told me of the dread you have of menial work. How you ran away from your previous master when you found out you were going to have to grind drabnat fruit.'

I snorted.

'There is a big difference,' I told him. 'For one thing, I had no choice in the matter of grinding fruit. I was to be chained to that wheel for life, like it or lump it. This would be something I *chose* to do, a way of thanking you and Mistress Sarah for helping me and keeping me warm and fed. And for another thing . . .'

He looked at me with interest.

'Yes?'

'I think I could be of use to you.'

'Really?'

He was smiling but he seemed to be taking my words seriously enough.

'In what way?'

'Well, Master, I like to think of myself as a pretty good judge of what's funny and what's not. I could advise you on your routines as we went along. I could help you hone and develop your material. And, not only that . . .'

'Go on,' he said.

'Well, you've often commented on the fact that talking animals such as myself are quite rare.'

'Certainly ones that talk as eloquently as you,' he agreed. 'And as relentlessly.'

'Quite! Think what a wonderful . . . oh, what's the word you use . . . grimmick, grommick . . . ?'

'Gimmick?' suggested Alexander.

'Yes, exactly! Whenever we approached a town or city, I could announce you! "This way to see Alexander Darke, the famous jester!" I would cry. I tell you, they'd come running like mutts after a straggler. Can you imagine a better way of publicising yourself?'

'I suppose not.'

Alexander looked thoughtful.

'So, what you're proposing is not just the usual master and beast relationship. It would be more of a . . . partnership.'

'A partnership,' I said quietly. 'I rather like the sound of that.'

'Well, then,' said Alexander. 'I think we have a deal, Max. We'll start first thing tomorrow morning. Which leaves you tonight to break the news to Betty.'

'I . . . beg your pardon?'

I looked at him in alarm.

'Me?' I gasped. 'Oh, but ... couldn't you do it, Master?'

But he was already out of the paddock and strolling towards the house.

'It'll be better coming from you,' he assured me.

It was one of the first occasions when I discovered that, charming as he was, there was a certain slippery quality to Alexander Darke. And he had dropped me right in the brown stuff.

Chapter 13

Breaking The News

The hours went by as I pondered my dilemma. Betty was a good friend and companion; I certainly didn't want to upset her, or make her feel that I had stolen her purpose in life. I couldn't bear to think of her being angry or resentful towards me. After all, hadn't she accepted me without hesitation when I'd been brought into her paddock? She had been so kind and generous and it seemed a mean way to repay her, by telling her that she was now surplus to requirements.

I fussed and fretted until I felt I could put it off no longer. Taking a deep breath, I walked quietly across the paddock and stood over Betty, watching her sleep. Then I cleared my throat, but that did no good at all. I prodded her flank gently with my snout. Nothing. I prodded her harder. Finally, with a grunt, she woke up and lifted her head to gaze blearily at me.

'Oh, Max,' she said. 'It's you. Whatever's wrong?'

'Betty,' I said. 'I apologise for waking you, but there's a matter of some urgency I must discuss with you. It's come to my attention that you've been looking very tired lately.'

She gave me a sharp look.

'You woke me up to say that I've been looking tired?' she said. 'Little wonder!'

'Er . . . yes, well, hear me out. I have decided that tomorrow morning, you should be allowed to have the luxury of a nice long lie-in.'

'I hardly think so,' she said. 'The master will be calling for me at first light, as he always does.'

'Er . . . well, no, there's the thing. I thought, tomorrow morning . . . just for a change, I would pull the caravan and leave you here to slumber in peace.'

'That's very thoughtful of you,' she said. ' You know, I wouldn't mind. . .'

She broke off and her eyes narrowed suspiciously.

'Just a moment,' she said. 'He's asked you to take over from me, hasn't he? The master has decided that I'm too old and broken down to pull that caravan any more.'

I began to panic.

'Er . . . goodness, Betty, whatever gave you that idea? No, we just thought, the master and me, that you had earned a bit of a breather. You know, a chance to get yourself back to your old fighting form.'

'Nonsense! He thinks I'm over the hill. He's trading me in for a newer, younger model.'

'Not at all, Betty, the very idea! Why, he just wants to . . .'

But I broke off as I registered the look on Betty's long and elegant face. It was an expression of sheer delight.

'About ruddy time!' she cried.

'I beg your pardon?'

'I thought he'd never ask. I've been struggling to pull that flipping caravan for the last year and, when you started getting to a decent size, I thought perhaps *you* might offer, but no, nothing was said, and I had to go on struggling well past the time when such work was within my capabilities. Now, finally, I'm getting the chance to have a rest. Hooray, that's what I say!'

I stared down at her in amazement.

'Then you . . . don't mind?'

'Mind? I'm delighted! Just be sure you don't make too much noise when you set off tomorrow; I'm planning on having a nice, long lie-in. Oh and a word to the wise, Max, you'll find that caravan pulls a little to the left; you'll have to compensate for that by leaning to the right. You'll get the hang of it in no time.'

'Umm . . . right then. No problem. I'll er . . . let you get back to sleep, shall I?'

'Okey dokey. And I'd get some rest yourself, if I were you. You've spent a long time lazing around. The first few days are sure to take it out of you. Goodnight, Max, and . . . congratulations.'

'Er . . . thank you.'

Within moments she had gone back to sleep and was snoring contentedly. I walked quietly back to the other side of the paddock. I had the distinct impression that somebody had just got one over on me, but I couldn't for the life of me figure out how they had done it.

I settled down on the ground and quickly fell into a deep, dreamless slumber. I seemed to be asleep for only moments; then I heard the sound of Alexander's footsteps approaching the paddock and I knew it was time for my new life to begin.

I wolfed down some food and took a good long drink of water from the trough. Alexander led me out of the paddock and buckled me into the unfamiliar harness that connected me to the caravan. When all was ready, he gave the reins a gentle twitch and I tested the weight of the caravan, remembering Betty's tip about pulling to the right. The caravan moved easily and we started for the track that led to the gate.

As we moved past the paddock, I stole a glance at Betty.

She was lying in her familiar sleeping pose, but, as we went by, I thought I saw that her eyes were half open and she was watching us go. And ... I could have been wrong, but it seemed to me that her eyes were sparkling unnaturally, as though they were heavy with tears.

But I could not think about that now. I was taking my master to his next engagement and there was a great distance to travel before we reached our destination. We were a team and now we had to work together to make Alexander a success.

Chapter 14

That's Entertainment

I don't wish to blow my own trumpet or anything, but it worked like a dream. Alexander's act had needed just one more element to make it different from all the other jesters' acts out there; *I* was that element.

Within just a few weeks of the two of us teaming up, his act was going down a storm, wherever he appeared. And I like to think that I played a major part in achieving this transformation.

Picture the scene if you will. A small market town, somewhere in the vastness of the great plains. A bustle of people moving around the various stalls in the town square, going through the monotonous routines of their everyday lives. Suddenly, heads lift in curiosity, as a brightly painted caravan trundles into the square, pulled along by a magnificent buffalope in his prime. (Me, naturally.) At the reins, sits a mysterious figure in multi-coloured clothing. And then, wonder of wonders, the buffalope lifts his handsome head and begins to proclaim in a voice that booms across the square.

'Ladies and gentlemen, boys and girls. Step right this way for the performance of a lifetime! Fresh from his triumphs in the palaces of Jerebim' (completely fictitious, this bit, but that's Show Business for you) 'I give you the Lord of Laughter, the Sovereign of Silliness, the Monarch of Mirth . . . yes, it's Alexander Darke, Prrrrrrrince of Fools!'

The title was my idea. Before that, he'd just been plain old Alexander Darke, but I had pointed out that his biggest rival in this field, the celebrated jester, Jonathan Jolly, billed himself as King of Comics, so we needed to give Alexander an equally regal title; it was I who urged him to have this title painted onto the side of the caravan, as a kind of travelling advertisement.

You see, if I have learned one thing about show business, it is this: you can't beat a big entrance. Alexander's routines weren't much different than they'd been before . . . oh, I'd honed them a bit, told him to dump a few jokes that, frankly, weren't up to scratch, but, other than that, his material was the same as it had been before.

But now, the arrival of the caravan was causing such a stir that people came to the performances in a more receptive state of mind, ready and eager to be entertained and, in that, my master did not disappoint them. When it came time to pass around the hat, he was finding to his delight that he was getting twice or even three times as much as before.

I, for my part, was enjoying this new life. I felt that I was doing much more than your average beast of burden; that I was, in fact, an integral part of the act. Of course, I had to play all this down when I returned to the paddock every evening and found Betty waiting for me, ready to hear about the latest adventure. Having taken her ease all day, she would be wide awake and now it was *I* who was desperate to get some rest; but I always made a point of telling her what had transpired that day, before turning in for the night. I thought it was the least I could do.

Of course, things didn't always go as smoothly as they might. I well remember the day that we pulled into the square of a grubby little village called Rotherpike and we were astonished to see another caravan, entering from the far side of it.

Alexander gave a groan of despair.

'It's Jonathan Jolly,' he said.

The caravan was pulled by a rather skinny grey horse

and seated at the reins was a dark-haired, bearded fellow who was so fat, he was almost bursting out of the red and yellow jester's outfit he was wearing. He was strumming a mandolin and singing in a deep, fruity baritone.

> *Greetings all you people*
> *Please step along this way*
> *The reigning King of Comedy*
> *Is visiting today*
> *With jokes and japes aplenty*
> *To brighten up your day*
> *So stop your toil and hurry*
> *It's time for us to play.*
> *I'm Jonathan!*
> *I'm Jolly!*
> *So give me all your lolly*
> *I'll make you laugh and cheer*
> *And shout hurray!*

'Hmph!' I muttered. 'He's not what you'd call a gifted singer, is he?'

'Doesn't matter,' said Alexander gloomily. 'Look at them running to his caravan!'

This was true enough. The populace was crowding around the Jolly caravan, as though their very lives depended upon it.

'It's just the song,' I protested. 'Anyone can have a song. Let's set up at the other side of the square and I'll introduce you. We'll soon see who can draw the biggest crowd.'

But the master shook his head.

'No sense in even trying,' he said. 'He's been pleasing crowds for years; he'd wipe the floor with us.'

'Well, there's nothing like confidence, is there?' I muttered. 'With an attitude like that, you'll never get to the top.'

But he wouldn't be pushed into a contest.

'Come on,' he said, 'we'll put this one down to experience. Let's move closer and watch his act. You never know, we might learn something.'

Reluctantly, I did as Alexander suggested, moving as close to the jester as the eager crowd would allow me. By the time we had found a suitable position, the big man was standing on the steps of the village fountain and was beaming down at his audience. I took an instant dislike to the man. There was something course and brutish about his demeanour and his costume looked as though it hadn't had a good wash in years. His tiny blue eyes were cold and crafty and I got the impression that behind the image of the knockabout fool, there actually lurked a rather unpleasant individual, who only had his own best interests at heart.

'Good to be back in Rotherpike,' he announced in a deep, rumbling voice that seemed to fill the entire square. 'Of course, this village has always had a special place in my heart, because this is where I met my wife all those years ago. You know, it's a wonderful thing to have the love of a good woman for twenty years . . . let's hope she doesn't find out about it!'

Much to my surprise, this poor opening joke was met with a chorus of hearty guffaws. He continued in a similar vein.

'You know, I still hold her hand wherever we go. That way, she can't do any shopping!'

He winked outrageously at the crowd and there was more laughter.

'Seriously though, it was our anniversary the other day. She said to me, "I'd like to go somewhere I've never been before." I said, "How about the kitchen?"'

More laughter. I looked around in astonishment.

'Master, he's just slagging off his poor wife,' I observed. 'Is that supposed to be funny?'

'Well, look at the audience,' said Alexander. 'They're lapping it up.'

This was true enough. The thing is, it wasn't just the menfolk who were finding this amusing; many of the ladies were nudging each other and having a cackle too.

'I decided to buy the wife something nice,' continued Jonathan Jolly, 'So I got her one of those new-fangled mud-packs. She looked great for two days. Then the mud fell off.'

Pause for breath.

'She complained of feeling ill so I took her to a doctor. He said, "I don't like the look of her." I said, "Neither do I, but she's good with the kids."'

Now the crowd was positively roaring with laughter and, I noticed, so was Jonathan Jolly. I didn't think it was good policy to be laughing at his own jokes, but the crowd didn't seem to mind. At last, he decided to switch subjects.

'A man wakes up one morning and discovers that his mutt has gone cross-eyed. He takes him to a vet. The vet picks up the dog, looks into his eyes and says, "I'm going to have to put him down." "Why?" cries the man. "Because he's cross-eyed?" "No," says the vet. "Because he's too bloody heavy!"'

Bellows and shrieks came from the audience now.

'By the way, what do you call a mutt with no legs? It doesn't matter; he won't come when you call him, anyway.'

Another brief pause and then he was off again.

'I met a pirate the other day. He had a peg-leg, a

hook for a hand and an eye patch. I asked him what had happened. He said, "I was swimming and a kelfer bit off my leg, so I had the peg-leg put on. Another time, I was reaching down into the water and another kelfer bit off my hand. So I had the hook put on." "What about the eye patch?" I asked him. "Well," he said, "I was on deck one day and a seagull pooed in my eye." I was amazed. "You lost an eye because of seagull poo?" I cried. "Not exactly," he said. "It was the day after I had the hook put on . . ."'

A brief pause ensued while the slow-witted audience thought about the joke . . . and then the laughter emerged, louder than before.

'A vampire bat comes back to his cave covered in fresh blood. All his mates want to know where he got it. So he takes them to the cave entrance and says, "See that big tree over there?" "Yes," they say. "Well, unfortunately, *I* didn't!"'

And so it went on, the seemingly inexhaustible supply of jokes being fired thick and fast to a very receptive audience. When he took his final bow, the applause was heartfelt and, when he came around with the hat, plenty of coins were flung into it. I noticed, however, that he left our caravan until the very last. When he finally approached us, Alexander dropped some croats into the hat.

'A masterly performance, Mr Jolly,' he said. 'You are indeed, the King of Comedy.'

Jolly gave a bow, but there was something decidedly mocking in the way he did it. As he straightened up, he paused to look at the words painted on the side of the caravan, and he raised his bushy eyebrows in mock surprise.

'A fellow comedian,' he observed. 'Prince of Fools, indeed! It would seem I have some competition.'

'Oh, not at all,' Alexander assured him. 'I am but a beginner in this line of work. Your reputation is known throughout the land, I would not even try to put myself at your level. But, everybody must start somewhere.'

Jolly gave Alexander a sly look.

'I suppose a prince is somewhat lower down the scale than a king,' he observed. 'You're admitting your inferiority in your very title. Little wonder you didn't dare to take me on.'

'Oh, it wasn't so much that I didn't *dare*,' Alexander assured him. 'It just seemed pointless to be adversaries, when there's the whole world to perform in. And, while a little healthy competition can be a good thing, there's no point in trying to shout each other down. That would be a pointless exercise.'

Jolly smirked.

'It seems to me that I have heard of you, Mr Darke.'

'Really?' Alexander smiled. 'Good things, I hope.'

Jolly examined his fingernails.

'Depends on your definition of *good*,' he said. 'I believe I was told that there was a new pretender travelling the country trying to pass off some of my old material as his own.'

'I can assure you, you are misinformed,' Alexander told him. 'I perform only my own jokes, Mr Jolly. Ones I have written myself.'

'Really? That's not what I was told.' Jolly laughed unpleasantly. 'A chancer from Jerebim, they said. Somebody who didn't have the first idea of how to tell a joke, yet determined to keep on trying to make a living out of it.'

I could hold my tongue no longer.

'How dare you suggest that my master would do such a thing?' I complained. 'His material is totally original, which is more than I can say for the sorry collection of wife-hating jokes I just heard you deliver.'

Jolly's eyes bulged and his mouth fell open. He stared up at Alexander.

'You're . . . a ventriloquist?' he asked.

'No, sir,' said Alexander, still trying hard to be civil. 'I have a buffalope with a quick tongue and an opinion, nothing more.'

Jolly's face turned a deep shade of red.

'Well, you ought to teach it to mind its manners and keep its opinion to itself. The ruddy cheek of it!'

He glared up at Alexander.

'You take my advice, son, and look for another line of work. There's only room for one jester in these parts and the post is already taken. I've been civil to you today but, if I see you again, I won't be anything like as nice. You got that?'

Alexander stared resolutely back at Jolly.

'I hear what you're saying,' he said. 'But there's room for more than one jester in the world, and I would rather we were friends than enemies.'

'Tough,' snarled Jolly. 'I don't need any more friends. You've been warned. Don't let me see you again.'

And, with that, he spun around on his heel and stalked back to his own caravan.

'What a charmer,' I observed. 'Honestly, Master, you should go and demand back the coins you just gave him.'

Alexander chuckled.

'I doubt that would do anything to improve his mood,' he said. 'He may be Jolly by name, but he's certainly not jolly by nature. A pity, it would have been better to be friends.'

He sighed.

'Come on, Shaggy, there's no point in trying to work

this crowd; they must be all laughed out. Let's head for home.'

He clicked the reins and I started moving out of the square.

'You're not going to take any notice of him, are you?' I asked, as we headed back along the road that led onto the plains.

'Certainly not,' he assured me. 'A man cannot claim exclusive rights to all the humour in the world. That's a ridiculous notion if ever I heard one.'

'If you can call it humour,' I said. 'I found a lot of it rather distasteful. You wouldn't make nasty remarks about Mistress Sarah, would you?'

'Well, no, but that kind of comedy can be very popular. You saw the way the crowd reacted . . . and lots of the audience were women.'

'Yes, Master, that's what makes it seem worse. How could they laugh when their whole species is being got at? It seems to me that humour of that kind is just plain nasty. I think you'd be well advised to steer away from jokes that attack.'

'Most comedy attacks *something*,' said Alexander. 'What about all the jokes I do regarding merchants?'

'Oh well, that's different,' I said. 'They deserve every-thing you can heap on them!'

Alexander chuckled.

'Hmm. I don't suppose this view is influenced by the bad treatment you experienced at the hands of a certain Berundian oil seller?'

I shrugged my shoulders.

'Possibly,' I admitted. 'But wives are precious things, Master. If I'm ever lucky enough to have one, I can assure you I won't go round saying bad things about her.'

This seemed to amuse him.

'Do buffalope take wives, then?'

'Of course they do. But I'm a bit young to be thinking about something like that.'

We walked along in silence for a while. All around us lay the barren wastes of the great plains – and I found myself thinking wistfully of the green, lush plains of Neruvia, where I was born. Not that I was unhappy where I was, but I would have liked to visit it again and of course, to see Mama, safe and well. But I didn't want to dwell on that; besides, the first stirrings of a great idea were forming in my mind.

'Master?' I said.

'Yes?'

'You know the way Jonathan Jolly arrived, just now? Singing that song?'

'What of it?'

'Supposing *you* had a song . . . a really brilliant one?

112

Funny, witty, full of tongue-twisters. You *can* play the mandolin, can't you?'

'Yes . . . but I don't know about writing lyrics. That's not really my strong point.'

'No problem,' I assured him. 'I'll take care of that little matter.'

'You . . . you can write songs?'

'Well, I've never really had occasion to try. But I feel sure that if I apply myself, I could come up with something suitably clever. Better than that fat oaf's caterwauling, that's for sure.'

'Hmm. Well, there's no harm in having a go, I suppose. But even if you *can* write a song, there's a more fundamental problem.'

'Which is?'

'My voice,' he said. 'I'm tone deaf, I'm afraid. Have been ever since I was a child.'

'Hmm. That's not the end of the world, either. Not when I have a very well modulated baritone, myself.'

'You . . . you can sing?'

'Oh, back in the herd, I was renowned for my renditions of the old buffalope songs. You should have heard my version of *Drifting On The Plains* . . . or the *Big Muddy Wallow* . . . though of course they would just sound like an unintelligible series of moos and grunts to you. I'm sure singing in the human tongue can't be any more difficult than that.'

Alexander didn't say anything else and I could tell he was having grave doubts about my abilities; but, if there's one thing I've learned over the years, it's this. A good buffalope can put his mind to just about anything and, nine times out of ten, he'll pull it off. The song was no exception. It took some time coming, but when it did, by golly, it was a belter!

Chapter 15

The Singing Buffalope

It took me a while but I finally had the song completed to my satisfaction. The problem was that I was unable to write anything down and had to keep going through it in my mind until I finally had it memorised. Of course, I also had to come up with a suitable melody and the only way I could do that was to hum various themes. I swear that Betty was starting to think that I had quite taken leave of my senses.

But finally, after many long nights of struggle, I felt that I had something worthy of Alexander. So, one evening, I summoned him to the paddock and, by the light of a lantern, I sang it for him. This is how it went.

Lads and lasses! Lords and Ladies!
Gather round and hear my song.
Humour lovers, fans of laughter

Step this way, you can't go wrong!
For here comes someone so fantastic
Oh so witty, such a lark . . .
Introducing, for your pleasure
The famous Alexander Darke!
He's outrageous! So contagious!
He will claim you heart and soul
He'll tell stories, to amuse you,
Dry and witty, oh so droll.
Jokes and riddles, comic capers
Are my master's ready tools.
Come and see him, long to be him
The one and only Prince Of Fools!

After I had finished, I looked at Alexander. He was sitting there on a bale of straw, staring at me. His mouth was hanging open and, in the poor light, I took his expression to be one of dismay.

'You . . . do not care for my song, Master?' I asked him.

He shook his head.

'No, Max, I do not *care* for it . . . I love it!'

His expression changed to one of delight.

'I just can't believe that you wrote it. I mean, goodness me, you haven't been talking much more than a year; how did you ever . . . ?'

'Oh, it's just a little ditty, Master, nothing to get excited about.'

'On the contrary, it's perfect. I'll go and get my mandolin and we'll work out the chords.'

He got up to hurry away but then paused, as though he'd just thought of something.

'You don't think . . . well, that you've laid it on a bit thick, do you?'

Now it was my turn to stare at him.

'Whatever do you mean, Master?'

'All those superlatives. I'd hate to be a disappointment to people.'

'Master, the whole point about these songs is to blow your own trumpet. I mean, Jonathan Jolly's song doesn't say, "Here comes a fat oaf with a bunch of third-rate jokes about women," does it? He wouldn't get much of a crowd if he told the truth, would he?'

Alexander smiled.

'I suppose not,' he said.

'And, likewise, we can hardly say about you, "Here comes a promising young jester, who once he's got more experience and boosted his confidence a bit, is likely to be quite amusing."'

Now he laughed.

'You're right,' he said. 'That wouldn't do at all. Max, what would I do without you?'

He hurried off to get his mandolin, leaving me to stand there, feeling rather smug. Then came a voice behind me.

'You seem to be doing very well in your new role.'

I turned to see Betty standing just beyond the light of the lantern. She had gone down a lot over the last few months; she was thin and shaky on her feet and I knew that she probably wouldn't be around for very much longer. In fact, it was unusual for her to be awake at this hour; but then, perhaps my singing had been a bit more raucous than I'd imagined.

'The master clearly liked your song,' she said. 'I wish I could understand the human words.'

'That's no problem,' I told her.

And I sang it for her in the language of the plains. It was an on-the-spot translation, but I think I got it across quite well. When I had finished, she nodded her head and snorted appreciatively.

'You're a very clever creature, Max,' she observed. 'You've done so much for the master in such a short space of time, more than I ever did in all my years of service to the Darke family.'

'Oh, I've done nothing,' I assured her. 'A silly song, a bit of advice; how does that compare to a lifetime of hard work?'

I was being uncharacteristically modest, but then, I

didn't want her to feel that she was in some way inferior. As I have said already, I had the highest regard for Betty – and it couldn't have been easy, watching a young pretender like myself taking over her duties and doing so well at them.

She fixed me with a look.

'Max, a word of advice, if I may be so bold?'

'Of course,' I said.

'A mutt may walk on its hind legs, but that doesn't make it human. Likewise, you have mastered the human tongue and you are doing things that I'm sure no other buffalope has done before you. But . . . at the end of the day, you are still a buffalope and you must never lose sight of that.'

'Thanks for the advice,' I said.

I must admit that, at the time, young and arrogant as I was, I didn't really understand what she meant. It was only years later, when I had grown into an adult, that her words came back to haunt me and I finally understood the wisdom in them.

It was one of the last things she ever said to me. Only a few days later, I awoke to see that she was lying in her usual place in the corner of the paddock. Alexander and I were leaving early in order to reach an appointment in a far-off town, so I left her sleeping. It was only in the evening when we returned, that I noticed she had not moved a muscle. I alerted Alexander and he went over to look at her. He crouched beside her, stroking her head gently and I knew by his grim expression what had happened.

'Her troubles are over now,' he said quietly and I just stood there, wishing there was something I could say to make it better.

Chapter 16

Three Strangers

In those early days we criss-crossed the length and breadth of the land to reach our various destinations. The caravan was heavy and I grew stronger and stronger as each day passed. We often met with other travellers along the way and, mostly, our experiences were positive ones; but not always.

I well remember one hot summer's day on the road to Bodengen, when we saw a cloud of dust up ahead and, after a while, we noticed three men, mounted on equines, riding slowly towards us.

My experiences as a youngster had made me understandably nervous about the approach of strangers.

'Master,' I said. 'There are humans approaching.'

'I've seen them,' he said calmly. 'Just keep on going.'

As the three strangers drew closer, my heart fell. They were one of the ugliest trios I had ever clapped eyes on. They were dressed in hides and furs and their bare arms and shoulders were covered with crudely executed tattoos.

'I don't like the look of them,' I said quietly.

'Me neither,' said Alexander, but still his voice remained calm. 'Brigands, no doubt about it. But say nothing and leave the talking to me.'

The three men drew their equines to a halt on the road in front of us and, for the moment, I could do nothing but pull to a halt. I was able to get a good look at their faces. The first man was bald and had evil, hooded eyes that made me feel very nervous. The second was squat and wizened and was grinning nastily, revealing that he had barely more than three teeth in his head. The last man was tall and thin and had a huge nose that stood out from his face like the beak of a huge bird of prey. In my mind, I instantly assigned them nicknames; Baldy, Gap and Beaky.

It was Gap who spoke first, his voice horribly distorted by his absence of teeth.

'Good morning to you, Sir,' he said, in a mocking tone. 'That's a fine caravan you have there.'

He ran his eyes over me.

'Pity you don't have a handsome equine to pull it along for you.'

'I'm happy enough with my buffalope,' said Alexander. 'He gets me wherever I want to go.'

'And where would you be heading on such a fine day?' asked Baldy.

'To Bodengen,' said Alexander. 'I'm a jester and I'm to do a performance there.'

The three men exchanged glances and Beaky sniffed.

'Like jokes, do you?' he growled.

'It would be a poor thing if I didn't,' admitted Alexander. 'I tell them all the time.'

'Well I've got one for you,' said Beaky. 'Did you hear about the jester who got robbed on the way to Bodengen?'

There was a pause before Alexander came back with his answer.

'No, I don't believe I know that one. Tell me, how does it go?'

Baldy laughed unpleasantly.

'Three strong lads meet with a jester. They make short work of him, take his caravan and his buffalope. Then they strip off his fine outfit and leave him for the vultures to pick at.'

Alexander didn't say anything for a few moments. He seemed to be considering what Baldy had said.

'That's not much of a joke,' he said, at last. 'It has no punchline.'

'A punchline?'

Baldy seemed offended that Alexander wasn't showing any evidence of fear.

'What are you blathering about?'

'Your joke. Forgive me, but it doesn't really work. Let me offer you a better version. Three stupid thieves meet with a jester on the road to Bodengen . . .'

'What did you say?' gasped Beaky.

'Shush, I haven't finished. The first thief is as bald as a drabnat fruit. The second is as ugly as a babarusa licking urine off a thistle. And the third has such a big nose that it should have been classed as a deadly weapon.'

'Why you . . .' snarled Gap, but Alexander held up a hand to silence him.

'The jester tells them that he can help each of them to be a better man. "How can we do that?" they ask. To the first man, he says, "Stick two rabbits on your head. From a distance they'll look like hares!" To the second man, he says, "Paint a face on your backside and walk on your hands; that will definitely be a big improvement." And to the third man, he says, "Don't change a thing. Just offer to shelter six children under your nose when it starts to rain."'

Alexander laughed.

'See, that's just off the top of my head, but it's a better joke than your poor attempt.'

Beaky scowled.

'It's the last joke you'll ever tell,' he said.

And, sliding his sword from its sheath, he urged his equine forward. His two friends followed his example. I braced myself to meet them with my horns, but I had no opportunity to do anything. I heard the hiss of steel behind me as Alexander drew his own sword and then to my surprise, my master's feet thudded down onto the broad expanse of my back.

There was a hiss of air and quite suddenly, Beaky's distinctive head was falling through the air and rolling across the ground at my feet. Before the others even had time to draw breath, Alexander had leapt from my back and jumped astride Beaky's equine, shoving the man's headless body aside as he did so.

Now he urged the creature forward, ducked a wild blow from Gap and stabbed the point of his curved sword into the ugly man's stomach, making him double over with a gasp of pain. Baldy urged his mount forward, trying to seize an advantage, but Gap's equine reared up between him and Alexander, blocking his sword thrust. Alexander urged Beaky's equine around in a tight circle and came at the remaining brigand with terrible ferocity, bringing the curved blade down deep into his shoulder and knocking him from his saddle. Baldy hit the ground hard and lay there, writhing in pain, clutching his bleeding shoulder. His look of apprehension told me that he was expecting the deathblow, but it never came.

Instead, Alexander snatched up the reins of the two other horses, kicked Gap's slumped figure out of the saddle and rode calmly around to the rear of the caravan, where I heard the sound of him hitching them in place. After a few moments, he came strolling back around to me, wiping his bloody sword on a handful of grass as he did so. He sheathed the sword and then climbed back into his seat. I stared back at him over my shoulder, astounded by the speed with which it had all happened. It was the first indication I had that my master, despite his placid looks, was evidently a master swordsman.

Baldy looked up at him in dismay.

'I'm bleeding!' he gasped.

Alexander studied him for a moment.

'So you are,' he said, sounding genuinely surprised. 'Cut yourself shaving, did you?'

'You . . .'

Baldy glared at him.

'This is no laughing matter,' he snarled.

'You seemed to think it was before,' said Alexander. 'When you were telling me how you were going to take my belongings. I distinctly remember you laughing.'

He picked up the reins.

'Where do you think you're going?' cried Baldy.

'I don't *think* I'm going anywhere,' said Alexander. 'I know I'm going to Bodengen. Forgive me, I thought I'd already told you that.'

'But ... you ... you can't leave me here like this. It's ... murder.'

Alexander glanced around for a moment.

'Oh, it's not that bad,' he said. 'A bit dull, but I've seen worse.'

'You know what I mean!' protested Baldy. 'I'm bleeding to death here! At least let me keep my equine.'

'Let me think about it,' said Alexander.

He paused for about one second.

'No, sorry, don't think so. I'd like to help, but you know what? You were planning to rob and murder me and – call me old-fashioned – but that doesn't exactly endear me to a person. So I think I'll sell the equines in Bodengen. Your friends have no further need of them and, judging by the look of you, you'll soon be joining them. Well, bye now!'

He flicked the reins, startling me, and I moved off, kicking Beaky's head gingerly out of the way as I did so. Behind us, I could hear Baldy's desperate yells, pleading with us to come back. I waited until they had faded into the distance before I spoke.

'Well, that was a surprise,' I said.

'Was it?' Alexander seemed amused. 'Thought I'd be a pushover, did you?'

'Well, forgive me, but I had no idea you were so talented with the sword.'

Alexander chuckled.

'My father was a sword maker and he knew very well how to use the weapons he made. He taught me well. He said to me, "Alexander, if you're intent on telling those terrible jokes and stories for a living, you'd better know how to defend yourself."'

'Your father wasn't too keen on your choice of profession, then?"

'No. He really wanted me to follow in his footsteps. I tried my best to please him, but I had no skill at making swords.'

'But plenty of skill at *using* them,' I said. 'He must have been pleased about that, at least.'

'Oh, I suppose so. But it's the duty of any father to teach a son how to bear arms. If I am ever lucky enough to have a son, I'll make sure he knows one end of a sword from the other.'

'I can't help feeling you're being modest. You just made mincemeat of those brigands.'

Alexander shrugged.

'I'm never one to start trouble,' he said. 'But I'm

only too happy to finish it. And I don't much care for bullies.'

We went on our way without any more problems and, after that, I felt a lot less nervous of strangers, whenever we encountered them. If there's something I've learned over the years, it's this: if you must have a master, it pays to have one who's a bit handy when it comes to trouble.

Chapter 17

Opportunity Knocks

I don't know if it was the song I had written, or whether my valuable input was giving the master more confidence, but the act finally began to take off. Whenever we arrived at a town or village, the populace would come running to see Alexander Darke, Prince of Fools. The laughter was that bit louder, the applause that bit more heartfelt and, when it came to passing around the hat, the returns were definitely up on previous visits.

To show his gratitude, the master started buying me little treats: rich, red pommers or a bucket of golden starfruit, all of which were gratefully received. I had as powerful an appetite then as I have today, which may account for my lifelong struggle with my figure.

We didn't know it, but the act was about to take a very important step up, one that would set Alexander on the path to real success.

We were in the town square of Jerebim, one day, where my master was performing his usual act for a packed and appreciative audience. As was my usual custom, I was positioned close by, so that I was on hand whenever he needed a voice to provide feed lines or to make announcements.

As the performance continued, I noticed a beautifully decorated sedan chair carried by four servants pushing its way through the crowd to the front of the stage, a sure sign that somebody of quality had arrived. The chair was duly set down in a good spot and one of the servants hurried forward to open the door.

A tall, thin man stepped out to view the proceedings. He was wearing an opulent purple cloak, a gold turban and enough jewellery to make him glitter in the sunlight, like the surface of a pool of water. He had a long, equine-like face, with a neatly trimmed beard curving down from his chin and as he stood there watching, his lips twisted into a wry smile.

I glanced at Alexander, but, as usual, he was so caught up in his routine, he didn't seem to have noticed this new arrival. I hoped that none of the material he was using would prove too vulgar for such a sophisticated viewer, but my worries were unfounded. As the show neared its conclusion, I noticed that the rich man was laughing heartily and, when my master took his final bow, he clapped his gloved hands together, to show his appreciation.

'And now,' I bellowed, 'my master will pass among you and relieve you of all those heavy coins in your pockets and purses!'

The rich man stared at me in evident astonishment for a moment; then he laughed again and reached for his purse. When my master came close to him, holding out his jester's hat, the man threw in a coin – not the usual croat, but a heavy gold crown. My master noticed this and bowed respectfully, before moving on.

The crowd began to disperse but the rich man remained where he was, watching as Alexander packed up his various props. Then he sauntered towards the stage.

'Mister Darke,' he said, in a slow, cultured voice. 'I must congratulate you on a most hilarious perform-ance. I have heard nothing but good things about your act and decided to come and judge for myself.'

Alexander bowed low a second time.

'You honour me, Sir,' he said. 'I try to please as wide an audience as possible.'

'And you succeed, admirably! Allow me to intro-duce myself. I am Lord Frobisher of the Royal Court of Jerebim, loyal subject and advisor to his Majesty King Cletus the Magnificent.'

'Ruddy Nora!' I said.

I couldn't help it, it just slipped out. I'd never been so close to royalty before.

Alexander gave me a wary look but Lord Frobisher seemed amused.

'That's a remarkable beast you have there,' he observed. 'I have been told that he performs a song at the start of your act but, sadly, I arrived too late to hear it.'

He cast a baleful look across to his servants.

'These curs will taste the whip when they get home for being so tardy.'

'Oh, don't do that!' I cried.

Lord Frobisher gave me a startled look.

'I beg your pardon?' he said.

'It's just that . . . well, I know what it's like to be beaten and I wouldn't wish that on anyone. If it pleases you, sir, I shall sing the song for you now and then there is no need to beat anybody.'

Lord Frobisher's expression darkened for a moment, but then he seemed to relent.

'As you wish, Master Buffalope. Pray, sing!'

So I did as he commanded, making sure I enunciated every word clearly and, by the time I got to the end of the song, Lord Frobisher was smiling and tapping his foot to the rhythm, like any robust villager.

133

'Splendid!' he said, as I took my own little bow. 'Quite clearly this beast is an important part of your act, Mr Darke. It is fortunate indeed that you found him.'

He glanced quickly around and then stepped closer, as if to confide a secret.

'I shall get straight to the point,' he said. 'His eminence the King has been, of late, in poor spirits. As you may be aware, his wife, your late Queen, has been dead some years and there has been nobody to replace her in his affections. He is, as I'm sure you know, the father of a thirteen-year-old son and, without the stability of a wife to guide him in that respect, has consequently been in a melancholic frame of mind for quite some time.'

Alexander nodded warily, perhaps guessing where this was going and feeling somewhat apprehensive about it.

'It has occurred to me,' continued Lord Frobisher, 'that his Majesty would benefit from some good old hearty laugher. That's where you come in. I propose to organise a birthday entertainment for his majesty, featuring the very best dancers, jugglers and of course, top of the bill, the funniest jester in the land. Now, there were some who assured me that one Jonathan Jolly was the man to approach . . .'

Alexander nodded good-naturedly.

'Mr Jolly does have a splendid reputation,' he said.

'A quite undeserved one, if you ask me,' said Lord Frobisher. 'I caught his act yesterday and I was far from impressed. Nothing but a bunch of abuse heaped on his unfortunate wife.'

'Hear, hear!' I said.

'I have to say, Mr Darke, that I thought you were much funnier.'

'You're very kind to say that,' said Alexander. 'But to play in front of the King? I'm not sure that I . . .'

'What my master is trying to say,' I interrupted hastily, 'is that he's not sure whether we might not already have a booking for the day in question. When is the King's birthday, exactly?'

Lord Frobisher looked affronted by my ignorance.

'In exactly seven days' time,' he told me. 'As any loyal subject would be able to tell you.'

'I knew that,' said Alexander quickly, but I was far from convinced.

'And Mr Darke, if you do have a booking for then, I would suggest that you change it, immediately! This is an incredible honour for any act . . . not to mention a handsome fee of three gold crowns!'

Again Alexander bowed.

'Your Lordship is too kind,' he said. 'That is surely far too much . . .'

' . . . to waste on an act as inferior as that of Jonathan Jolly,' I finished. 'We look forward to the performance and will do our utmost to bring laughter to our beloved king, of that you can be most sure.'

Alexander threw me a furious scowl but I ignored it. Some people just don't want to be helped. Lord Frobisher reached into his handsomely embroidered tunic and pulled out a piece of parchment, bearing the wax seal of the Royal Court.

'Splendid,' he said. 'Be at the palace gates prompt at noon in seven days' time and show this pass to the guards. And mark you, Mr Darke, ensure that you perform only your most hilarious routines. I want to see his Majesty recover his good spirits. Then he might look favourably upon some projects I have in mind.'

I might have known there'd be an ulterior motive. Humans rarely do anything out of the goodness of their hearts.

Lord Frobisher turned away with a swish of his purple cloak.

'Until seven days' time,' he said, and climbed back into his sedan chair.

We watched as the servants lifted the device from the ground and swung around in the direction of the palace. One of them mouthed a silent 'thank you' to me as they struggled by.

We waited until Lord Frobisher was out of earshot.

'Thanks a heap,' muttered Alexander, at last. 'I was doing my best to get us out of that.'

'Yes, and I can't imagine why. Hear that knocking sound? That's opportunity, that is and you must always answer a call like that; you'd be crazy not to.'

Alexander frowned.

'I don't know,' he said. 'The Royal Court of Jerebim? I've never appeared anywhere so grand in my life. Supposing the King doesn't like me?'

'Of course he'll like you!' I told him. 'You'll have me with you for a start-off and *everyone* likes me. You saw that Lord Frobisher's face when I was singing. It looked like he was about to soil his breeches.'

'Well, thank goodness he didn't,' said Alexander.

He reached into the hat he was holding and plucked out the gold crown.

'Imagine,' he said. 'He'll pay us another three of these. Sarah will be delighted; we'll be able to buy the proper table and chairs she's been wanting.'

'That's the spirit!' I told him. 'We're going up in the world, Master. We're playing for the quality now. If the King finds you funny, who knows where it might lead?'

Alexander sighed.

'And if he doesn't find me funny?'

'Honestly, you're a terrible worrier,' I said. 'It's going to be brilliant, you just wait and see!'

Chapter 18

A Rival

But it didn't take long to discover that not everybody was as pleased by our good fortune as I was. Only the following day, as my master was performing on a makeshift stage outside a tavern in the town of Glumm, there was a sudden commotion amidst the audience and a familiar burly figure came pushing and shoving his way through the press of spectators. He was dressed in the distinctive multicoloured uniform of a jester.

'What the bloody 'ell do you think you're playing at?' bellowed Jonathan Jolly.

My master broke off in mid joke and gazed down at his enemy for a moment in surprise. Then he recovered himself.

'Ladies and gentlemen,' he announced, calmly. 'We are honoured to have a special guest with us today. Mr Jonathan Jolly, King of Comics.'

A few people in the crowd started to applaud but were cut short by Jolly's reply.

'Don't try and worm your way out of it with smart remarks,' he cried, climbing the two steps to the stage. 'I've heard about your underhand dealings. Just who do you think you are?'

He turned to address the crowd.

'This snake in the grass has stolen my chance to perform for King Cletus!' he told them. 'Yeah, that's right. On our beloved King's birthday. It should have been me, but no, it will be this upstart instead.'

'Nobody has stolen anything,' Alexander assured them. 'Lord Frobisher viewed both of our acts and decided that mine was the one the King would most enjoy. It was as much a surprise to me as it clearly has been to Mr Jolly. But nothing underhand went on.'

There were murmurs and nods of assent from the crowd, but Jolly wasn't so easily appeased.

'Who in his right mind would choose your miserable excuse for an act over mine?' he protested 'Everyone knows, I'm the funniest jester in all the land and I have been for twenty years.'

'Yes,' I quipped, from the side of the stage. 'Unfortunately you're still using the same jokes.'

This caused a ripple of laughter amongst the crowd, but Jolly clearly wasn't amused.

'And as for that fleabag,' he said, pointing down at me, 'I don't know how you can stand being in the same place. I mean, aren't you aware of that awful stench?'

'Yes,' said Alexander. 'But stay right where you are, Mr Jolly, I'm sure we'll all get used to it.'

There was more laughter from the crowd, stronger now. Jolly's eyes bulged and his flabby face turned a deep shade of crimson.

'Why you . . . don't try and match your wits with mine, Darke, because you'll only make yourself look stupid. I could out-joke you under the table.'

'Perhaps,' I told him. 'But wouldn't you be more comfortable standing up?'

Again the crowd responded. Jolly stared resentfully around at them for a moment.

'Hah!' he sneered. 'I don't know what you lot are laughing at.'

'It's called a joke,' I told him. 'You should try telling one yourself sometime.'

'You call that a joke?' He grinned wildly around at the audience. 'Here's one for you,' he said. 'What's fat, stupid and full of wind?'

'Oh, don't be so hard on yourself,' said Alexander; and the crowd erupted into laughter once again.

'I didn't mean *me*,' snapped Jolly. 'I was talking about that buffalope! He . . . he thinks he can tell jokes as good as any man.'

'Not *any* man,' I assured him. 'Just you. Mind you, that's not difficult.'

I turned my head and winked at the crowd.

'You know, Mr Jolly was born on a farm . . . I wonder if there were any more in the litter?'

'I'm not saying he's ugly,' said Alexander. 'But when he comes into a room, mice jump onto chairs.'

'His wife keeps a portrait of him on the mantel-piece,' I said. 'It keeps the kids away from the fire.'

'He was planning to kill all the people who disliked him . . .' said Alexander. 'But they said it would be genocide!'

'Mind you,' I added, 'he still loves nature, despite what it did to him.'

'And talk about stupid,' said Alexander. 'If ignorance is bliss, he must be the happiest man alive!'

Jolly tried to splutter something in his defence but, having seized the opportunity, we weren't going to let it pass us by.

'We *could* make him look stupid,' I said. 'But why should *we* take all the credit?'

'If he had an original thought it would die of loneliness.'

'He doesn't know the meaning of fear – but then, he doesn't know the meaning of *most* words.'

'If brains were gunpowder, he wouldn't have enough to blow his hat off.'

'If brains were taxed, he'd get a rebate.'

'If you gave him a croat for his thoughts, you'd be owed some change.'

I almost felt sorry for Jolly. He was being blasted from either side with no chance of getting a word in edgeways. By now the people in the crowd were laughing out loud at him and he didn't like it one little bit.

'Shut up a minute!' he roared at them. 'Shut up, I say!'

He waved his arms at them until they quietened down.

'Why don't we put it to the vote, eh? Those who think I'm the funniest jester, say *Aye*.'

There was a long damning silence.

Then somebody in the crowd shouted, 'Get off, fatso, we want to watch the rest of the act.'

Jolly reeled back as though he had been punched.

'Who said that?' he yelled, pacing up and down. 'Step forward whoever said that and I'll knock your bloomin' block off! How dare you insult the King of Comics?'

'The King of Crap, you mean,' shrieked an old crone in the crowd. 'Shove off and let's hear the Prince of Fools!'

'You stupid old ratbag!' yelled Jolly. 'Who cares what you think?'

Now boos and jeers were coming from the crowd. Jolly was working himself up into a real frenzy and didn't seem to realise that he was simply inviting the crowd to turn against him.

'What do you morons know about comedy, anyway?' he roared. 'I was on the road cracking jokes when most of you were in your cradles! You ingrates! I've entertained you for years. Years! And this is the kind of thanks I get. You really think these two are funnier than me?'

'AYE!' There was no hesitation; the reply came back loud and strong.

'Imbeciles!' he roared. 'You don't deserve me!'

A piece of ripe fruit came whizzing out of the crowd and splattered against Jolly's colourful tunic with a dull plop. He stared down at it in dismay.

'Who threw that?' he bellowed. 'Step forward who did that and apologise.' Nobody did.

'If you lot throw one more thing, I'm leaving and I'm never coming back . . .'

Alexander's eyes widened in alarm and he ducked

quickly behind one of his prop baskets. It had been a wise move. As if at an unseen signal, a fusillade of objects came flying from the crowd – fruit, stones, handfuls of mud, whatever came to hand. Jolly's colourful figure became even more so as a barrage of soft items splattered him from head to foot. As a final insult, a fresh cowpat came hurtling over the heads of the onlookers and hit him full in the face.

The crowd fell suddenly silent, feeling perhaps that they had gone too far. Jolly stood there, the fresh dung running down his face and steaming in the sunlight.

'Right,' he said. 'That does it.'

He stepped down from the stage and pushed his way through the crowd. A great cheer went up as he walked away. I gazed after him, almost with a sense of sadness. Jonathan Jolly had just learned a powerful lesson. Never disrespect your audience.

I don't know what happened to him after that. Perhaps he moved away. Perhaps he gave up jestering and became a farmer or a blacksmith. Who can say? I only know that I never heard tell of him again.

As for my master, he emerged from his hiding place to enthusiastic cheers and went on with his act, as if nothing had happened. But afterwards, when he was packing away his props, I saw that he looked sad and I asked him what was troubling him.

'I hope we weren't too hard on Mr Jolly,' he said. 'For all his faults, he was an accomplished jester.'

That was Alexander Darke for you. Such a forgiving nature. It sometimes made me wonder how he ever expected to get on in life.

Chapter 19

By Royal Appointment

The King's birthday approached and my master seemed to grow more anxious with each passing day. He rehearsed and rehearsed his act, trimming out any material he was not one hundred per cent happy with. I am proud to say that I was of great assistance in this. Every joke that went into the Royal Performance had to pass 'the Max test': that is to say, if it didn't strike me as being at least mildly amusing, it was thrown out.

Meanwhile, Sarah washed and pressed Alexander's finest outfit (a rather dashing number featuring black and yellow diamonds), she cut his hair so that it hung neat and straight to his shoulders and she insisted that, the night before the performance, he should have a bath, immersing his whole body in hot water, which she painstakingly heated over an open fire out in the yard.

She then produced a bar of scented soap, which she had procured from a Berundian merchant and she directed my poor master to apply it to himself. He emerged from the bath smelling like a flower garden in midsummer. I was trying not to laugh, when I noticed Mistress Sarah gazing thoughtfully at me and I quickly made myself scarce, not wishing to suffer a similar fate.

On the morning of the King's birthday, Sarah prepared my master's favourite breakfast of fried gallock eggs and javralat rashers, while she provided me with a bucket of sweet red pommers. If I close my eyes, I can still taste them, even after all these years.

When Alexander came out to the stable, dressed in the colourful but rather tight-fitting costume, I asked him if he'd enjoyed his breakfast, to which he gloomily replied that the condemned man had eaten a hearty meal.

'Oh come now, Master, don't you think you're being a bit pessimistic?' I asked him. 'King Cletus has a reputation for being fair and just. I hardly think he'd chop somebody's head off simply because he didn't find the jokes very funny.'

But Alexander didn't seem convinced. He harnessed me to the caravan and, when we were ready to set off,

Mistress Sarah came out to bid us farewell. She smiled at the apprehensive look on her husband's face.

'You'll be fine,' she assured him.

'I hope so,' he said, dismally.

He leaned down from the seat and gave his wife a tender kiss.

'If anything bad should happen, you'll find a farewell letter in my props room.'

'It won't come to that,' she assured him. 'King Cletus is going to love you. I know he is. Now get going; you don't want to keep him waiting, do you?'

Alexander shook his head. He flicked the reins and we set off along the road to Jerebim, both of us aware that today's performance would either make or break Alexander in his chosen career.

After an uneventful journey, we found ourselves moving through the bustling streets and narrow thoroughfares of Jerebim and, as we went, I could hear Alexander going over and over his material, as though terrified that he might forget something.

'Relax,' I told him. 'If you make yourself too nervous, you're more likely to get something wrong. Just imagine you're outside a rowdy tavern in some little market town.'

'That's easily said,' he moaned, 'but not so easily done.'

At length, the huge stone walls of the King's palace reared up before us and we made our way to the main entrance, where a couple of heavily armed guards regarded us suspiciously; but, when Alexander produced the parchment with the King's seal, they stood aside and called for the gates to be opened.

We passed through into a scene of much excitement. A large stage, decorated with brightly coloured silk flags, had been erected in the palace grounds and rows of wooden seats had been arranged in front of it. In the very front row stood a magnificent throne, decorated with gold leaf and carved figures, and we instantly knew that this was where King Cletus would be sitting, almost close enough to reach out and grab my master's leg if he chose to. Beside the throne sat a smaller child-sized version, which I knew must be for the King's teenage son, Daniel.

This was the point where I would normally be singing my introduction but, as yet, there was no audience in sight, so we decided to keep it for later. A couple of attendants instructed me to guide the wagon around to the side of the stage, so that my master could unpack his props. He did so, where we found the two support acts, a juggler and a tumbler, already preparing themselves for the performance. As was his way, Alexander chatted to the two men and wished them luck; but, as he set about unpacking his props, I could tell that he was far from happy with the proceedings.

'What about your song?' he muttered. 'It's part of the act now. I don't like leaving it out.'

'Perhaps I could sing it from down here?' I suggested.

'Yes, but then the audience won't *see* you. That's what makes it so funny, when they see this wonderful song coming from the mouth of a buffalope.'

'What's so funny about that?' I asked, but he ignored the question.

He looked thoughtfully at the short flight of wooden steps leading up to the stage.

'Do you think you could get up those, Max?' he asked me. 'Then you could sing the song standing beside me, while I accompanied you on the mandolin.'

I snuffled.

'No problem, Master. It's but one small step for a buffalope, one giant leap for buffalope-kind.'

I thought for a moment and then I had a brain-wave.

'Master, I have a better idea! We shall walk out onto the stage with you playing the mandolin and I singing as you ride upon my back. Can you imagine what a showstopper that would be?'

Alexander frowned.

'It does *sound* good,' he admitted. 'But we've never tried that before; we'd better rehearse it.'

I was just nodding my head in agreement when a figure appeared from around the front of the stage. It was Lord Frobisher, striding forward in his imperious purple cloak.

'Ah good, you're all here!' he observed, which struck me as a rather stupid remark, but I didn't comment on it. 'Is everything in readiness?'

'Yes, my Lord,' said Alexander. 'We were just going to try a quick . . .'

'Never mind!' Lord Frobisher waved a hand impatiently. 'The Lord and Ladies of the Royal Court are about to take their seats.'

He surveyed the three performers sternly.

'I'm sure I don't have to tell you that, as organiser of this occasion, my reputation is on the line. I would therefore suggest that all three of you perform to your very best ability. Do that and there'll be an extra gold crown for each of you.'

'Thank you very much, my Lord,' I said and he gave me a quizzical look.

'I don't think he was including you,' whispered Alexander. 'Your Lordship, if I could just ask that we be allowed to . . .'

But then there was a loud fanfare of trumpets and

152

Lord Frobisher turned away with a swish of his cape and disappeared around the front of the stage. We heard a rising hubbub of voices as the guests appeared from within the palace and took their seats. Alexander shook his head.

'Too late to rehearse it now,' he said. 'Perhaps we should forget the new idea.'

'Are you kidding?' I cried. 'It'll be stupendous. Don't worry, we'll just busk it. After all, it's a simple idea; what can possibly go wrong?'

Once again, the trumpets sounded, a great blasting fanfare that announced the arrival of somebody of great importance. Alexander ran up the steps to the curtains at the side of the stage and peeped out.

'It's the King,' he called down to me. 'He's taking his seat on the throne.'

'How does he look?' I asked hopefully.

'A bit grim, to tell you the truth. He doesn't look the sort to suffer fools gladly.'

'We'll be fine,' I assured him.

'Now the murmuring of the crowd settled down and we heard Lord Frobisher's voice speaking out in a loud and clear tone.

'Your esteemed Majesty, welcome to this, your special birthday entertainment, organised by your most loyal and abject servant, that is to say, my good self, Lord

Quentin Frobisher. Without further ado, may I announce for your pleasure, the finest juggler in the land, Mr Andy Dextrous!'

And with that, Mr Dextrous, a short and rather plump little man with a bald head and a pronounced gap in his teeth, came striding out from the wings juggling eight gallock eggs as he did so. After a short interval, we heard polite applause, but Alexander, still peeping through the curtains did not seem to be reassured.

'The King looks bored,' he told me. 'He barely clapped for that trick. He looks like he'd rather be somewhere else.'

And so it continued all through Mr Dextrous's act. At length, he came off stage, sweating copiously and looking none too happy.

'Tricky crowd, that,' he told us as he went past.

Alexander gave me a doubtful look and I did my best to reassure him, even though I was feeling far from confident myself.

Next, Lord Frobisher's voice announced Thomas Trimble, the tumbler, and Mr Trimble walked onto the stage balanced atop a large round ball. He then proceeded to put himself through a series of leaps, twists and bodily contortions that suggested his limbs were made of rope. By now, I could not contain my own curiosity and I climbed the steps in order to peek through the curtains myself.

There was Thomas, giving it everything he'd got, and there was the audience, clapping politely at his every move, and there was King Cletus, a tall, thin man with a sallow face and prematurely grey beard, looking as though he was attending a séance. His thin mouth was permanently down-turned and, though he clapped when all the others did, it was completely without enthusiasm.

If the King looked fed up, the boy sitting beside him looked positively suicidal. He was stick-thin, pale, and the face that peered out from a curtain of lank, black hair looked as miserable as a wet weekend in the village of Glumm.

'The King's son doesn't exactly look a laugh riot,' I observed.

'Daniel the Doleful, they call him,' muttered Alexander. 'Apparently he never got over the death of his Mother.'

'He'll probably appreciate a good laugh then,' I said.

Alexander just shook his head.

'We're doomed,' he muttered. 'Do you think anybody will notice if we just sneak out of here?'

'Don't be ridiculous!' I told him, trying to keep the

tone of rising desperation out of my voice. 'It's going to be brilliant. You'll see.'

But then I saw Thomas Trimble's frustrated expression as he came off stage, balancing a table, a chair, a candlestick and a bread roll on various parts of his anatomy.

'Good luck,' he told us as he went by. 'You're going to need it.'

I heard Alexander take a sharp intake of breath and I tried to look casual – not an easy expression for a buffalope, but I did my best. Alexander ran to get his mandolin and then vaulted up onto my back. I stood there waiting, then heard a rather worried-sounding Lord Frobisher making his final announcement.

'And now, your Majesty, it's time for er . . . a little laughter. It is with great pride that I announce the star of this afternoon's performance, who, I'm sure, will . . . will lift your spirits. I give you the Master of Mirth, the Lord of Laughter, the High Priest of Hilarity. Fresh from his triumphs across the known world, a big welcome please to . . . Alexander Darke: Prince Of Fools!'

Chapter 20

On With The Show!

The 'big welcome' turned out to be a half-hearted ripple of applause. They didn't exactly put themselves out.

Alexander struck the opening chord on his mandolin and I launched into my song, whilst striding purposefully forward onto the stage.

'Lads and lasses, Lords and ladies!
Gather round and hear my – whoaaaaaahhhhhhh!'

Personally, I blame the carpenters. In their desire to please the King, they had sanded and polished the wooden boards to perfection. To a hard-hooved creature like myself, it was akin to stepping out onto the surface of a frozen lake. My feet could get no purchase and, because I had launched myself forward with such gusto, I found myself skidding uncontrollably across the stage.

I tried desperately to back pedal my rear legs in an attempt to slow myself down, but this simply had the effect of spinning me around. I heard Alexander yelling at me to stop, but he might as well have asked me to grab the wind and knit it into a fine bonnet for his wife.

As I span, I caught a glimpse of the audience's faces, moving from left to right across my vision, each one frozen in a look of astonishment.

Oh well, I thought, *at least it can't get much worse.*

Then one of my horns snagged in a line of bunting, pulling it tight. Unfortunately, the bunting was attached to a large piece of scenery, which pulled free from its moorings and came crashing down on top of my master's head. The canvas ripped and fell around his head and shoulders, jerking him backwards off me and leaving him hanging several feet above the stage, his thin legs pedalling furiously.

As I swung around to look back at him, I started trying to run towards him, but could only manage to run on the spot like a lunatic, and then my rear end collided with another piece of scenery at the far side of the stage. The canvas was pushed backwards for quite a distance and I fully expected it to rip and send me flailing backwards off the edge of the stage. But it must have been made of strong stuff, because it suddenly snapped back again, sending me whizzing towards Alexander. Unhappily, the tips of my horns caught in the legs of his trousers, wrenching him headlong out of the backdrop and depositing him face down on my back, his head virtually jammed up my rear end.

But now, at least, my trajectory was slowing and I thought that there might be some chance of rescuing the situation. I carefully repositioned myself to face the crowds and started to sing again.

> *'Lads and Lasses, Lords and Ladies*
> *Gather round and hear my song. . .'*

I was somewhat perturbed as I sang to hear a strange accompaniment. Not the mandolin that I was used to, but a series of strange creaks and groans. I was dimly aware of my master, scrambling around on my back in a very undignified way, as he tried to position himself facing the crowd. By some miracle, he had managed to hang onto the mandolin, and he struck a chord, but the recent events had served to put it horribly out of tune and what emerged sounded like some panther that had had its tail slammed in a door.

I tried to continue nonetheless, now even more aware of that strange creaking sound.

> *Jokes and riddles, comic capers*
> *Are my master's ready tools.*
> *Come and see him, long to be him*
> *The one and only Prince Of . . .*

And that's when the stage collapsed beneath me and sent me plunging into a ragged hole. I fell a short distance and then my feet thudded onto the ground beneath the stage, leaving just my head and the top of my back still sticking up from the hole. The impact of my landing made Alexander bounce up into the air. He came down hard and tipped backwards. The mandolin went flying out of his grasp, his legs flew up and there was a ripping sound as his tight trousers tore asunder. The high and mighty audience was then treated to an unfamiliar sight; my master's bare bottom.

There was a collective gasp of horror and then, mercifully, Alexander tipped sideways and rolled off my back. He hit the wooden boards and lay there gasping for breath. I stared in mute horror at the faces of the audience; in fact, I had no choice in the matter, because I was wedged in position. A silence settled, so deep,

160

so intense that I could hear Alexander's ragged breathing as he fought to control his mounting terror.

In that moment, I felt terrible. It had all gone hideously wrong and there was nobody to blame but myself.

And then, most unexpected of all, I heard the sound of laughter.

I looked down in astonishment to see that it was coming from King Cletus. The formally dour monarch was pointing at the stage and laughing as though he was about to bust a gut, laughing so hard that the tears were literally streaming down his face. Beside him, Daniel looked as miserable as ever and was staring at his father with a bemused expression on his pale face.

King Cletus made a valiant attempt to recover himself, but failed. He spluttered, chortled, then threw his head back and howled.

The members of the Royal Court turned to look at him in surprise; then, as they began to see that he was genuinely amused by what he had just seen, they began to join in with him, first just one or two, then more and more until, at last, the whole crowd, with the single exception of young Daniel, was roaring with laughter.

Amazed, Alexander got back to his feet, holding his torn trousers together with one hand and looking down at his audience in bewilderment. Now the King was applauding like crazy, slapping his hands together so hard, I feared that he would damage them.

'Bravo!' he roared. 'Master Jester that was the funniest thing I ever saw! The way you orchestrated all that chaos. Incredible! Lord Frobisher, where on earth did you find them?'

Lord Frobisher was on his feet now, bowing obsequiously and basking in the warmth of the King's praise.

'My Liege, I caught their act a short while ago and hoped they would be to your taste, but . . .'

'To my taste! They are superb. I haven't had such a laugh in years. Such wild abandon, such incredible timing. I want them to perform for me often!'

Now Alexander was trying to pull me up out of the hole, whilst desperately shielding his bare buttocks from the audience. My frantic attempts to lever myself back out on to the stage seemed to start the King laughing all over again and this, in turn, started the others laughing, until the courtyard was echoing to the sounds of hilarity.

I finally managed to get myself out onto some strong floorboards and Alexander and I took several bows, before picking our way across the wrecked stage to the safety of the wings. We were forced to return for several more bows before the noise finally subsided.

*   *   *

When Lord Frobisher found his way to us at the side of the stage, Alexander was in the caravan, slipping on a spare pair of trousers. I called him out and he came and stood in the doorway.

Lord Frobisher bowed to Alexander and he couldn't seem to stop smiling.

'Mr Darke, I must confess I'm astounded. I had expected to see the act that I saw in Glumm the other day, which was certainly comical enough, but this performance surpassed all expectation. How on earth did you know that his Majesty was so fond of physical comedy?'

Alexander grinned wildly.

'Oh, it's common knowledge, is it not? I'm sure I must have heard it somewhere.'

He glanced at me, as though seeking help on the matter.

'That's why we . . . er . . . devised this new routine,' I added. 'Because we wanted to please his Majesty.'

'Look,' said Alexander, 'I'm sorry if we were a bit rough on the stage and everything . . .'

'Oh, that doesn't matter! You put King Cletus in a good humour for the first time in years and that is a minor miracle in itself. You're obviously a very clever man, Mr Darke.'

Alexander smiled.

163

'Well, to be honest, we work as a team, sire. It er . . . took both of us to devise that routine.'

Lord Frobisher gave me a look and nodded.

'Quite so, quite so.'

He pulled a purse from his pocket and tossed it to my master.

'There, Mister Darke . . . and er . . . Mr Buffalope . . .'

'Max,' I said. 'My name is Max.'

'Ahem! Yes, quite. There are five gold crowns for your trouble. Yes, I know I promised you four if you performed well, but his Majesty was *so* delighted, I feel the extra is merited. Furthermore, his Majesty has asked me if you will indulge him on a regular basis – shall we say, once every two weeks?'

Now Alexander's grin spread across his face.

'We would be honoured,' he said, with a gracious bow. 'Please give his Majesty our profound thanks.'

'Excellent. It's decided then. I shall send a messenger to hammer out the details. Now, I must go. His Majesty has agreed to listen to a pet project of mine. So, you see, my little entertainment has had far-reaching consequences. I shall trust in you both to keep him sweet in the months to come. Farewell for now.'

And he swept away in his usual imperious manner. Alexander felt the weight of the purse in his hand.

'I don't quite believe it,' he said, 'but it appears to

have gone brilliantly. Max, once again, I am in your debt. I mean, it was your idea to go onstage like that. Had we done our normal routine, who knows what might have happened?'

I shrugged my shoulders.

'A happy accident, Master, nothing more. I just hope that King Cletus doesn't expect us to be quite so physical *every* time we go on stage!'

We enjoyed a hearty laugh over that remark. Neither of us could wait to get home and tell Mistress Sarah about our good fortune; but, after a little discussion, we both agreed not to tell her the full story.

Chapter 21

Rising Stars

From that day on, life changed for my master and me. When news of the success of the Royal Appearance got around, we were suddenly in great demand. It seemed that every Lord and Lady in the land wished to see the act that had so delighted King Cletus. Alexander even went so far as to have the words 'By Royal Appointment' added to the design on the side of his caravan.

Realising that the King had a soft spot for slapstick, we took great pains to devise more physical bits of comedy to add to the routine. To be honest, we never did anything quite as extreme as our debut performance, but King Cletus seemed equally entranced by the jokes and riddles that my master told, so that was no great problem. Every two weeks, we had a slot reserved to appear at the Palace and we always got a warm welcome, at least from the King. I had hoped that Daniel might eventually warm to us but, if anything, he seemed to dislike us more and more with every passing day and would sit through each performance with a scowl on his face.

It worried me, that. I remember discussing the matter with my master one fine afternoon as we returned from the Palace.

'Master,' I said. 'I hope you do not think it amiss of me to give you a word of caution.'

'Of course not,' he said.

'It's young Daniel the Doleful. He clearly does not share his Father's enthusiasm for our act.'

'Yes, I'm aware of that. But it's not a problem, surely?'

'Not *now*, Master. But King Cletus is not a young man and he won't always be around.'

'Hmm. I see your point. You're saying we could lose our Royal patronage one day. But . . . what can I do about the situation?'

'If I were you, I would try and find out what the boy *does* find funny . . . and incorporate it into the act, as quickly as possible.'

To be fair to my master, he did heed these words and for a time, he tried to experiment with different kinds of humour; but nothing seemed to appeal to Daniel; he was just a miserable little wretch and who

167

could worry about one small boy, when everybody else seemed to be clamouring for us?

Of course, as the money began to roll in, life for Alexander and Mistress Sarah changed beyond all recognition. My master was able to settle all of his outstanding debts and now he could afford to purchase some of the luxuries of life that had thus far been denied him.

He bought clothes and jewels for Mistress Sarah and he had the good sense to plough some of his earnings back into the act, buying better, more elaborate costumes and props. He even had a special cabinet built by master craftsmen in the town of Jerebim, an ingenious device with a hidden chamber at the back, which made it appear that whoever had stepped into the cabinet had disappeared into thin air. He incorporated this into the act, choosing a young lady from the audience and trusting her not to reveal how the trick was achieved and as far as I am aware, not one of them ever told on him.

The name of Alexander Darke now carried the same power that Jonathan Jolly once had; but, as I often had cause to wonder, where was Jonathan Jolly now? Nobody had heard of him for a long, long time and, it seemed to me, that what had happened to the former famous jester was a cautionary tale that my master would do well to heed. No matter how high a star may fly, eventually it will reach its highest arc and then start to fall.

My master's fall began a long time before his success started to diminish. He was at the very height of his career when he first discovered the lure of the demon drink. It happened like this . . .

We did an afternoon performance at an archery tournament in the market town of Mindleflange and, sharing the bill with us, was a conjurer called The Great Sensimo.

He seemed an affable enough fellow, able to perform some quite astonishing tricks and illusions, though I couldn't help noticing that, for such a young man, he had a very red nose and quite a few exposed blood vessels on his cheeks – the unmistakable signs of a man who is fond of alcohol.

However, he and the master seemed to get on like a house on fire and, after the performance, Sensimo suggested that he and Alexander might pop into a local tavern for what he referred to as a 'swift flagon'.

At first, Alexander politely declined the invitation, saying that he wanted to get back to his wife, but Sensimo was insistent and, eventually, Alexander gave in. He instructed me to tow the wagon to *The Mutt and Thumbscrew* and to wait for him outside, which, at first, I was glad to do. But I had not anticipated how long he would be in there.

It was fully dark when he came staggering out, with one arm wrapped around Sensimo's shoulders. He was laughing and talking in a very loud voice and I watched sadly as he and Sensimo went through an elaborate routine of bidding each other goodnight, which seemed to consist of pushing each other in the chest and sniggering at some obscure joke. Finally, Sensimo went staggering away to his own carriage and Alexander dragged himself into the seat and gave my rump a hard slap with the reins.

'Home!' he barked, as though he was talking to some common beast of burden.

I turned my head and fixed him with a look.

'You're drunk,' I said.

He glared at me.

'What if I am?' he snapped, in a slow slurred voice. 'It's no business of yours. Move on!'

I should explain.

There are some people who should never drink alcohol. This is something I have learned over the years. You take one man, for instance, who has a few drinks, gets a bit merry, sings a few songs, falls asleep and wakes up with a headache. No great problem there.

That's the category *I* fall into. I'm a model citizen when I have a bit of ale.

But then, you take another man. *He* has a few drinks and he just turns mean, nasty, spiteful and rude. Nobody knows why this should be the case. It just happens to certain people. And, I'm sorry to say, that my master fell into the second category. This was the first time I had ever seen him like this, but sadly, it wouldn't be the last.

Now he slapped me again, harder than before.

'Come on!' he said. 'Move it.'

I did as I was told but I wasn't about to leave it there.

'Mistress Sarah will be worried about us,' I told him. 'She was expecting us back in daylight.'

'Oh, she'll be all right. That woman can look after herself. Goodness, don't I work hard to earn her some money? Surely she can't begrudge me just one night to let my hair down?'

'I'm sure she doesn't begrudge you anything,' I said. 'But perhaps if you'd sent word to tell her you would be late back . . .'

'What's it to do with you?' he snarled. 'Who are you, anyway, my blessed wet nurse?'

I cannot deny that I felt particularly hurt by this jibe. After all, my remark had been prompted by concern for him, nothing more.

171

'I was under the impression that I was your partner,' I told him. 'However, it would seem I'm speaking out of turn, so . . .'

'Oh, lighten up, will you? C'mon, let's sing a little song to lift our spirits. We'll do the Alexander Darke introduction song. A one, two, three, FOUR!'

And with that he launched into a raucous, out-of-tune version of the song I'd written, seemingly unaware that I wasn't joining in with him. After a while, his singing trailed away and was replaced by a series of rasping snores.

It was a long and difficult journey across the plain in the moonlight and I was on edge all the way, looking nervously around whenever an owl hooted or a luper howled. And what would we do if we had an encounter with brigands? My master's brilliant swordsmanship would be of no avail if he couldn't even stand up.

But luckily we made it home without any trouble. As we neared the homestead, I was not surprised to see Mistress Sarah standing out on the front doorstep and anxiously holding up a lantern.

'Alexander!' she cried, as we drew nearer and he woke with a start. 'Where on earth have you been? I've been worried sick!'

'Oh, don't you start,' muttered Alexander, half climbing, half falling down from his seat. 'Goodness me, a man stops for a swift flagon for once in his life and all he gets is earache! Well, I'm going to bed!'

He stumbled past her into the house, leaving her standing there, looking stunned. She stared at me accusingly.

'What's been going on?' she asked.

'It's not my fault, Mistress,' I assured her. 'It was the magician who lured him into the tavern. The Great Sensimo, he's called. The Great Drunken Oaf might be a better name for him. I just waited outside . . . for ages!'

Sarah relaxed a little.

'Ah well,' she said. 'It's not as if he does it very often. In fact, now I come to think of it, I can't remember him ever doing it before. I suppose he's earned himself a bit of relaxation; he's been working hard. Both of you have. Here . . .'

She took hold of my bridle and led me towards the barn.

'You must be tired. Let's get you unhitched from the caravan.'

'I'm sorry, Mistress, my master usually does this job before he goes inside. It's surely not a task for one as delicate as yourself.'

She smiled.

'I expect I'll survive,' she said.

PHILIP CAVENEY

She swung open the door of the barn and hung the lantern up inside. Then she led me in and began to unbuckle the harness. I gave a sigh and shrugged my shoulders. It was always a good feeling when the harness came off. It reminded me of my younger days on the great plains, before I even knew what the humans were all about.

'I've prepared your supper already,' Mistress Sarah told me.

She looked thoughtful for a moment, then turned to look at me with those enchanting elvish eyes.

'Max, I don't suppose I've ever said this to you before, but I'm very grateful for the way you look after Alexander.'

'I, Mistress? Oh, I don't do so very much . . .'

'Of course you do! It's not just that you pull that great big wagon all over the plains, but . . . well, I know you've done so much to help him attain his success. The songs, the advice. . . I mean, Betty was a wonderful loyal creature, but she couldn't have helped him as you have and I thank the stars that he found you when he did.'

She rubbed my head affectionately and planted a little kiss on my cheek.

'I hope you'll always be around to look after him,' she added. 'Now . . . enjoy your supper!'

And she went out of the stable, leaving me to eat, which I did without any hesitation.

But, as I ate, I thought about what had happened tonight and I couldn't help but worry a little. Alexander had seemed like a different man with a few drinks inside him . . . a man I did not really care for.

I only hoped that there would be no repeat of the incident.

But, of course, this was only the beginning. At first such happenings were few and far between, but it would only take some fellow-performer to suggest a quick drink, a rakish Lord plying him with wine in an attempt to get the performance to go a bit longer, or some sycophantic fan who longed for the glory of saying that he had drunk a few flagons with the Prince of Fools . . . and there I would be, waiting impatiently outside some seedy tavern, imagining Mistress Sarah home alone, wondering what time we would return.

Pointless to try and lecture him when he was under the influence: then you'd get nothing but verbal abuse for your trouble. The following day of course, he'd be mortified, embarrassed, he'd swear to you that it would never happen again, that he'd never touch another drop of ale as long as he lived.

But, as time went on, it happened more and more and I was powerless to stop it.

As a consequence, life at the Darke household became somewhat strained. There were mornings when Mistress Sarah came out to see us off and insisted on talking to me, rather than her husband.

'Max,' she would say. 'Please tell your master that I will expect to see him while there is still some light left in the day.'

I would then have to repeat the phrase to Alexander, as though he hadn't actually heard what she had said.

'Max, kindly tell the mistress that I have no intention of staying out past nightfall, and that such an occurrence will only ever happen if my employer *insists* on me staying for a drink.'

'Max, please tell your master that no man can be persuaded to drink unless he already has a mind to!'

'Max, tell the mistress that some men are driven to drink by the constant nagging of their wives!'

'Max, tell the master that some women are driven to nagging by the drinking of their husbands!'

'Max, kindly say goodbye to the mistress for me.'

'Max, please bid the master a fond farewell and tell him that I love him very much.'

And so it went on. The happy times that I had enjoyed in my early days with the Darke family seemed to be slipping further and further away from me and I would have done anything to get them back again. But, if I have learned one thing in my life, it is this. When somebody has set out along the path to self-destruction, there is very little that you can say or do to make them turn back again.

Chapter 22

A Royal Enemy

Sometimes, danger can come from an unexpected direction.

We had just arrived for one of our regular perform-ances at the Palace and I was dismayed to learn that the Great Sensimo was one of the support acts. This inevitably meant a long session at the tavern afterwards and I had the foresight to suggest to Alexander that he send a messenger to warn Mistress Sarah. Thankfully, he took my advice and despatched a man straight away.

The show started on time. Sensimo walked out and did his magical tricks to quite warm applause, but it was my master whom everyone had come to see and, when he stepped out onto the stage, the applause was tumultuous. After the disaster of my first appearance, I had learned that it was best to stay in the wings and watch proceedings from there.

As ever, King Cletus was positively howling with laughter and, beside him, young Daniel was as pale and grim as ever. It must have been a constant annoyance to Alexander that he could never win the boy over, and today some reckless quality within him made him single Daniel out for ridicule. As soon as he started, I felt it was a mistake.

'Look at the face on him!' said Alexander, pointing to the boy. 'You know, when he was born, the doctor took one look at his face and slapped the midwife!'

King Cletus thought this was hilarious and so did the rest of the court, but Daniel just sat there, glaring daggers at the stage. This would have been a sensible moment to move on, but Alexander had got the bit between his teeth and continued in the same vein.

'Mind you, his father is devoted to him and takes him everywhere . . . but that's just so he never has to kiss him goodbye!'

Again, howls of laughter from the King and the court, but a cold, glassy-eyed stare of hatred from the boy himself. I began to hope that my master would move on to another subject. But he didn't.

'You know, young Daniel once tried to enter an ugly contest, but they told him, "No professionals!" He visited a haunted house and came out with an application form! King Cletus took him to the zoo and the man at the door said, "Thanks for bringing him back!"'

'Master!' I hissed through the curtain. 'Enough!'

Alexander must have heard me because he paused for a moment and then swung off onto another subject; but Daniel's expression remained the same and I saw that his little hands were bunched into fists. It struck me then that, whereas before Daniel had simply found Alexander unfunny, now he had reason to hate him. I resolved to warn my master about it.

But, as it happened, I had no opportunity to do that. No sooner had Alexander taken his final bow, then Sensimo was there to slap him on the back and suggest that they partake of the usual 'swift flagon'. So off we trooped, our vehicles riding side by side so the two men could 'chat' ('swap boasts' might be a better way to describe the conversation!) and, before very long, we arrived at the nearest alehouse, a rather more salubrious place than usual called *The King's Head*, which, because of its proximity to the Palace, boasted a painted portrait of King Cletus above the door. In marched Alexander and Sensimo and I was left to while away the time, as darkness descended.

I tried making conversation with Sensimo's skinny black equine, Roger, but even in the common language of the plains, he was no great shakes and had little of interest to say for himself.

The place where we had been left was absolutely packed with carriages and wagons of all shapes and sizes and was bordered by a long, tall hedgerow. For some inexplicable reason, Alexander had tethered me to a hitching post in front of the hedge. Perhaps he thought that I would get bored and attempt to make my way home, and I have to say that, after only a short while of trying to coax some conversation out of Roger, I might well have considered it.

I decided to make the best of things and grab some shuteye. We buffalopes are adept at sleeping standing up. I don't know how long I slumbered, but I was just having a lovely dream about eating my way through a huge orchard full of pommers, when I was somewhat surprised to be woken by the sound of a carriage pulling to a halt on the other side of the hedge. Then I heard the sound of a door creaking open.

'Your Highness,' said a deep, gruff voice, speaking in a hushed tone. 'I came just as soon as I received your message. This is my friend, Viktor, who is also your most loyal subject. Like me, he eagerly awaits the day when you ascend the throne.'

The voice that answered was that of a child. I had never heard Daniel the Doleful speak, but the voice was slow and mournful and the conversation had left some pretty big clues as to who had just arrived.

'Mark you, gentlemen, the tavern before you,' whispered Daniel in a cold and malevolent tone that quite belied his tender years. 'A popular drinking establishment, with which I am sure you are familiar. In there, an enemy of mine sits drinking. An insolent cur of a jester who dares to make mock of your future King.'

There was a brief pause and then a second man's voice said:

'Impudent swine. You wish us to teach him a lesson, sire?'

'More than that,' said the child's voice and I was shocked by the hatred in it. 'I wish you to end his miserable life.'

There were gasps of surprise from the two men.

'But sire, is it not the case that this man is a great favourite of your father?'

'What of it?'

'Well, if he were to discover that we were responsible for killing him, it would go badly with us.'

'My father shall not know. This will be our secret. You shall take the jester in the darkness when he returns to his caravan. You shall mask your faces and you will slay him quickly and cleanly, then flee before anybody discovers his body. Do this for me and this shall be yours.'

I heard the clink of a money purse and there was a pause while one of the men weighed it in his hands.

'A goodly sum, sire,' said the first man. 'But, with respect, not worth forfeiting our lives should anything go wrong.'

'This is only an initial payment,' continued Daniel. 'When I ascend to the throne, I will be ready to reward those who have been of special service to me. Land and property will be mine to dispense and those who have pleased me will be top of the list. I have two splendid estates in mind for you.'

Another pause, then the first man spoke.

'Then I think we have an understanding, sire.'

'Good. I must go now, before I am recognised. Wait till the jester is drunk. I am told he is over-fond of his ale and he will surely put up no resistance. You will know him by his brightly coloured costume.'

'It shall be done, Sire,' said the second man. 'Trust in us.'

'One other thing. The jester's caravan is pulled by a great stinking brute of a buffalope, one that talks rather too well for my liking. Let's send him to the same place as his master, just in case he should happen to witness the killing.'

'As you command, Sire,' said the two men together.

Then there was the sound of the carriage door closing, the lash of a whip and the carriage moving away. I stood there, fighting the urge to run.

'I wouldn't like to incur the wrath of that one,' I heard the first man say. 'He may be only a youngster, but he's chock full of venom.'

I heard the sound of a dagger sliding out of its sheath.

'Shall we find the buffalope and do him first?'

I swallowed nervously.

'No, let's wait till the jester makes his way back to his caravan. Then we can take them both together and be out of here before anybody knows what's happened. Come, we'll position ourselves so we can see the entrance of the tavern.'

Footsteps crunched away across the grass.

I stood there, fighting against a rising sense of panic. I had to warn my master! But there I was, tethered by the reins to a post and there was no way I would be able to untie the knot. I inched closer and tried chewing the thick leather reins.

'Oh come on,' said Roger, 'you can't be that hungry!'

I ignored him. He spoke no human and clearly hadn't understood any of the conversation that I had just over-heard. I didn't seem to be making much impression on the reins so, impatient to be free, I hunched my shoulders and began to move backwards, pulling on them as hard as I could.

Roger gave me an affronted look.

'What are you doing?' he asked me.

'What does it look like?' I snapped. 'I'm trying to get free, obviously.'

The leather reins were stretched to their fullest but they refused to snap. The wooden rail began to creak under the pressure.

'Stop that!' said Roger. 'You'll damage the rail and then I might get into trouble.'

'You think *you're* in trouble,' I told him. 'Believe me, you don't know the meaning of the word.'

I continued to exert a slow, powerful pressure, putting all my strength into it and finally, with a loud crack, the wooden rail snapped in the middle and the reins came free. Unfortunately, a section of rail swung up and rapped Roger on the snout.

'Oh, that's lovely, that is!' he snickered. 'I hope you're pleased with yourself.'

'Roger, do belt up!' I advised him.

Now I was trying to manoeuvre myself backwards so I could get the caravan out from the vehicles that flanked me. The caravan swung to one side and bashed into Sensimo's wagon.

'*Now* what are you doing?' complained Roger.

'My exercises,' I told him. 'I'm trying to lose weight, aren't I? This is called the caravan workout. Now please shut up and let me concentrate. Ah . . .'

At last, I had backed out far enough to make a turn and head towards the tavern.

'Where do you think you're going?' shrieked Roger. 'You can't go to the tavern; you're a beast of burden.'

'I'll go wherever I please,' I told him. 'And stop making so much noise; you'll attract attention.'

'Huh! Not as much as you will,' was his final remark. 'A buffalope going into a tavern? Who ever heard of such a thing?'

I couldn't worry about that now. I had other things on my mind.

Chapter 23

A Close Shave

I moved cautiously towards the tavern, trying not to trip over the reins, which were trailing on the ground beneath me. I reminded myself that the killers had said they would position themselves where they could watch the entrance. With this in mind, I veered to my right, across a stretch of grass, noticing as I did so that there was a window at the far end of the building and that the thick wooden shutters were open.

I made my way towards it, aware that the heavy metal-rimmed wheels were churning deep tracks into the soft ground. I made it to the window, from which the sound of music, laughter and the strong smell of ale spilled. My view was somewhat obscured by a young couple who were standing in the window, kissing and hugging each other in a most improper fashion. I stood there politely for a moment and then, growing impatient, I cleared my throat.

They jolted apart as though I had kicked them and stood there staring at me, their mouths open.

'Excuse me,' I said. 'Sorry to interrupt and all that, but would you mind shifting out of the way? I'm looking for somebody.'

They did as I asked, still staring at me as though they couldn't quite believe their eyes. I stuck my head in through the open window and peered at the press of bodies in the smoke-filled interior but I didn't see Alexander's distinctive costume anywhere.

'I was looking for Alexander Darke, the jester,' I told the couple.

The young man nodded and pointed to his right.

'Oh I . . . I think he's in the snug at the back,' he muttered.

'Right, thank you. Here, do me a favour will you? Pick up these reins and drape them over my back. I'm in danger of falling over them.'

The young man leaned out of the window and did as I asked, while the woman watched him entranced, as though he was performing a magic trick.

'Thanks,' I said, when he had finished. 'Sorry to interrupt. Please carry on with what you were doing.'

I walked on to the end of the long building and

peered around the corner. Luckily there was another window back there and, once again, it was open. I trundled my way along to that and peered in. Sure enough, there sat Alexander and Sensimo at a table piled high with empty tankards, chortling away at some joke and clearly already well on their way to total inebriation.

'Master!' I hissed. 'Master!'

Alexander lifted his head and glared at me.

'What do you want?' he growled.

'I just wanted to tell you that . . .'

'Clear off, will you? I'll come out when I'm good and ready.'

He looked at Sensimo, as though seeking back-up.

'I mean to say, a chap can't even enjoy a couple of ales without some wet-nurse of a buffalope pestering him.'

'Master,' I said, 'you don't understand. There are people out here who . . .'

'Where I come from,' slurred Sensimo, 'buffalopes know their place. You wouldn't find one sticking his head through the window and giving orders.'

'I'm not giving orders!' I cried. 'I'm just trying to warn my master . . .'

'Yes, yes!' cried Alexander. 'Mistress Sarah will be worried about me. Well, I'm sick of hearing about it.

I've already sent a messenger to warn her; what more d'you want? Blood?'

And with that, he got up from the table and staggered towards the window.

'Master,' I said. 'I only want to tell you . . .'

And then he slammed the wooden shutters of the window in my face. I stood there, staring at them in disbelief. The ingratitude of the man! For a moment, I fully intended to head for home and leave him to his fate but, after a few moments' reflection, I realised that I couldn't do that. No, I would have to think of something and the only idea that came to me was the thought of causing some kind of diversion.

I looked quickly around and noticed an oil lantern hanging from a hook on a wall not far from the shuttered window. On the ground, a short distance away from it there was a large stack of kindling and some empty ale barrels. I looked from the lantern to the stack, gauging the probability of getting the aim right. It didn't seem too difficult. I approached the lantern and lifted my head carefully until the tip of a horn fit through the hook from which the lantern was hanging. Then I gave my head a quick, hard flick to the right.

The lantern came off its hook and performed a slow, lazy arc through the air. Then it crashed down onto the pile of wood, flinging its contents all over the stack.

There was a sudden 'whump' as the flames ignited and almost instantly a great cloud of smoke drifted up against the wall of the tavern.

I swung around to my left and ran back to the other window, where I saw that the young couple had resumed their frantic canoodling. Not waiting for them to move, I shoved my head past them and bellowed 'FIRE!' as loud as I could. The noise of it made the young couple drop to the floor in total shock and, looking past them, I could see a sudden wave of panic passing through the drinkers within, as clouds of smoke came drifting from the direction of the snug. There was a general commotion as people threw down their tankards and flagons and headed for the door.

There was no time to waste! I pulled my head back out of the window and galloped on along the wall, heading now for the main entrance, the caravan bucking and shuddering behind me. As I got to the front of the building, I saw a frantic press of people already spilling out of the open doors and, off to one side, two villainous-looking men, daggers drawn, inspecting each person as they went by. As I drew closer still, I saw Alexander and Sensimo amidst the crowd, clearly confused and the worse for wear with drink.

The taller of the two assassins spotted Alexander's

multi-coloured costume and, grabbing his companion by the arm, he pointed. They began to move forward.

Now I had a problem. The crowd was moving between me and the killers and there was every chance that they would get to my master before I could. For a moment, I was about to check my speed, but then I realised that I just couldn't do that, so I opened my mouth and I bellowed as loud as I could.

'Get out of the way!' I roared.

Happily, the column of people reacted, parting in front of me like waves on either side of a rock, leaping out of the way as I thundered towards them. Alexander and Sensimo stood there, staring at me as though I had lost my mind and, for a terrible moment, it seemed as though I would trample them into the ground. But then Alexander must have noticed the two sinister-looking men moving towards him and he grabbed Sensimo's arm and the two of them stepped back out of harm's way.

I missed the two of them by a hair's breadth and raced past, with the assassins firmly in my sights. I saw the look of horror they gave me, the way the colour drained abruptly from their faces, and then I lowered my horns and ploughed into them. At the last instant, I lifted my head and the two men went flailing up into the air like a pair of rag dolls, slamming onto the roof of the caravan and bouncing off again. I didn't wait around but turned the caravan in as tight a circle as I could manage and headed back towards the tavern, slowing my pace as I did so.

Alexander was standing there, staring stupidly at the two moaning shapes I had left heaped in the grass.

'Get on,' I told him.

'But . . .' he began.

'Hurry!' I said. 'Those men are assassins, paid to kill you!'

He didn't say anything to that, just clambered unsteadily up to his seat and grabbed the reins.

Sensimo stood there staring up at him.

'You're not leaving already, are you?' he slurred.

'Yes, he ruddy well is!' I snapped and took off as fast as my legs would carry me.

'But . . . it was *his* round!' I heard Sensimo yell.

'I expect you'll survive,' I called back.

Then I was heading out onto the road beyond the tavern and going like the clappers in the direction of home.

Once we were out on the open plain, I finally felt safe enough to slow down to a walk. Alexander was showing all the signs of falling into a drunken stupor but I wasn't going to let him get away that lightly.

'You can't go on like this,' I told him.

'What do you mean?' he said indignantly. 'Go on like what?'

'You know perfectly well. There were two men back there who had every intention of gutting you like a fish. Me too, for that matter.'

'Oh, I could have handled *them*,' said Alexander, trying to sound casual. 'I'd just have pulled out my trusty sword and given them the old one-two!'

'Don't make me laugh,' I said. 'The old one-two? I doubt that you could count that high in your condition. You can barely stand!'

'I can handle my drink,' he said defensively.

There was a long pause and then he said, sheepishly, 'But thanks for your help.'

He thought for a moment.

'Who were they, anyway?'

'Two villains hired by Daniel the Doleful,' I said. 'I overheard him giving them instructions; a good job, too, otherwise you'd have had no chance. Clearly he took exception to the remarks you made about him at the performance today.'

'What? Those little jokes about him being miserable and ugly? Bit of an over-reaction, isn't it?'

'Master, if you'd had your full wits about you, you'd never have gone down that road in the first place. I mean, criticising the son of the King! It's a good job His Majesty saw the funny side of it. He could have had you thrown in the dungeons. It's a side-effect of the drink; it's affecting your judgement.'

'Nonsense! I have it under control, I tell you.'

Another silence, while he brooded on what I had told him.

'Well, clearly I'll have to have a quiet word with King Cletus about this.'

'You'll do nothing of the sort!' I said.

'Why ever not?'

'Master, do you know of any man who would take the word of an entertainer over that of his son? You go marching in there, making accusations, and you can say goodbye to your Royal Performances, once and for all.'

'You really think so?'

'I'm sure of it.'

'But what's to say the kid won't try something like this again?'

'Nothing, Master. But forewarned is forearmed. We'll just need to have our wits about us and keep an eye peeled for trouble. And that means you'll need a clear head and an un-addled brain.'

'Yes; do you think for once we could avoid the lecture?'

'I'm serious, Master. Let's not forget that, one day, King Cletus will be gone and his son will be sitting on the throne in his place. What do you suppose are the chances he'll decide to let bygones be bygones and invite you over to crack a few jokes?'

Alexander frowned.

'That's a good point,' he said. 'I hadn't even thought of that.'

'Yes, well, luckily, Master, I'm here to do that for you. You'd do well to have a plan worked out for exactly what you'll do when King Cletus pops off to meet his maker. He's not a youngster; it could happen any time now.'

'Yes, thanks for that! And listen, Max, not a word of this to Mistress Sarah. She'll only worry.'

'Yes, Master. But I want you to promise me that you'll try . . . *really* try to steer clear of the taverns and alehouses. For both of our sakes.'

Alexander sighed.

'Very well,' he said. 'I'll turn over a new leaf. You'll see, after today things are going to be different.'

Chapter 24

Maximus

To be fair to Alexander, things *were* different for a few weeks. He made a real effort to steer clear of the taverns and he positively avoided the company of people like Sensimo, who he knew had the knack of tempting him to indulge himself in drinking.

The Royal Performances continued and Alexander was most careful not to pick on young Daniel again; but, from my regular place at the side of the stage, I could see that the boy's stare was as filled with icy hatred as ever. We kept ourselves wary, particularly whenever we were in some lonely spot, but no more attacks transpired and we both began to relax our guard a little.

Inevitably, as the threat of danger seemed to pass, so Alexander's resolve weakened and, gradually, he began to slip back into his old ways. He just couldn't seem to help himself.

The problem was, when he was drinking, his judgement wasn't sound. Take Maximus, for instance. How my master ever ended up buying him is something I still haven't fully made sense of.

It happened like this.

We'd just finished a show in the town of Skelton, a modest place famous for its homemade pies and pastries. On the journey home, Alexander directed me to take a route, which I knew would bring us past one of his favourite drinking dens. I found myself hoping that he'd be able to resist the impulse to stop but, sure enough, as we drew close, he told me that he might just pop in for a quick drink. I tried arguing that it was late, that the mistress would be expecting us, all the usual stuff, but to no avail. He had a powerful thirst and he was not to be denied.

As we pulled in to the grounds, I noticed a thin, wiry-looking fellow lounging against a wall. He had sharp wolfish features, a long chin that ended in a black goatee beard and he was dressed in the flamboyant silk turban and velvet cloak of a prosperous merchant. I noticed that he was holding a leather riding crop in one gloved hand, which marked him out as a trader of equines; sure enough, only a short distance away, several of the beasts were tethered, browsing the grass at the side of the road.

As I came to a stop, the man nodded to Alexander and gave a supercilious little bow.

'As I live and breathe, 'tis the famous Mister Darke,' he said, in an oily voice. 'The celebrated Prince of Fools. I am a most devoted fan, sir.'

Alexander returned the bow.

'You are most kind, Mr . . . ?'

'Thynne. Josiah Thynne at your service. "Honest Josiah", as I am known far and wide.'

He made another obsequious bow and then stepped closer and studied the caravan for a few moments. He ran a gloved hand across the painted title on the side of the caravan.

'A fine vehicle, you have here,' he observed, 'worthy of a man of your esteem.'

Then he cast his cold grey eyes over me, and his smile faded.

'What a pity about your choice of steed.'

Alexander climbed down from the wagon.

'Oh, Max may be no oil painting, but he has his uses,' he said, dismissively.

'I'm sure he has,' agreed Josiah. 'Buffalopes are sturdy creatures, no doubt about it. Practical. Dependable. It's just that they lack a certain . . . shall we say, sense of style?'

I snorted.

'I'll have you know I'm considered very stylish amongst the buffalope fraternity,' I said. 'I was the first in my herd to wear my hair this way.'

Josiah stared at me.

'A talker, eh? Well, that is unusual. And no doubt it has a certain comic value. But surely Mr Darke, a man of your reputation deserves a more . . . *noble* beast to take his act around the country? Something with flair.'

He indicated the small group of equines a short distance away.

'Now, you look at Maximus there.'

He indicated the biggest of the beasts, a rather proud and superior-looking black stallion, who was taller and more heavily muscled than his companions.

'Sixteen hands tall, fresh from the great plains of Neruvia, a handsome beast who would turn the heads of everyone who saw him.'

'Max has his own way of turning heads,' said Alexander. 'He sings. I bet your fine equine can't do that.'

'No . . . but some creatures are so magnificent they do not need to advertise their qualities. The look is everything. It reflects on the man that owns him.'

'Thanks for your interest,' said Alexander, 'but I think I'll stick with old shaggy here.'

He slapped me on the flank.

'I won't be long,' he said.

'You are going inside?' Josiah asked him.

'Er . . . yes, just for a . . .'

'Swift flagon', I muttered.

Both men turned to look at me.

'That must take some getting used to,' said Josiah.

Then he put a hand on Alexander's shoulder.

'You know, I was just contemplating going in for a drink myself. Perhaps you would honour me by allowing me to buy you a tankard of ale.'

'That would be most kind,' said Alexander.

'Excellent, let us go in then.'

The two men walked towards the tavern entrance and I noticed how Josiah kept one hand on my master's shoulder, as though somehow claiming him as his own personal property – and the way he flung a sardonic smile over his shoulder at me.

I had a bad feeling about this. Once Alexander had a few ales inside him, his resolve would weaken, just as it had over the matter of not taking a drink. Still, I reasoned, no matter how drunk he was, he would never betray his partner, would he? There was nothing I could do for the moment, except wait.

As ever, the hours dragged themselves slowly by, and I was on the verge of falling asleep when I finally heard my master approaching. I glanced up and my heart sank. Alexander was walking with the kind of exaggerated care that regular drunkards employ in a vain attempt to make people think that they're still sober.

Beside him, Josiah Thynne was walking and talking like somebody who had drunk nothing more affecting than a glass of water. I noticed that he was clutching a money purse in one gloved hand. As I watched, he detached himself from my master and went across to the group of equines. He untied the reins of the one called Maximus and led him around to the rear of the caravan.

'I'll just tie him to the back here,' he announced. 'He'll follow you along quite happily.'

'Yes, whatever!' slurred Alexander.

I looked at my master in despair.

'You've bought the equine?' I cried in disbelief.

He shrugged his shoulders.

'I may have. What's it got to do with you?'

He was as churlish as ever he was when he was steeped in alcohol.

'But . . . we don't need him. What will we do with him?'

'He'll pull the caravan, of course.'

I stared at him. 'Pull the . . . but . . . that's *my* job!'

Alexander waved a hand.

'It's time you had a bit of a break,' he said. 'You've earned yourself a rest.'

Josiah came back to the front of the wagon.

'A pleasure to do business with you, sir,' he said, in that disagreeably oily tone. 'I'm sure you'll be very pleased with Maximus. But don't forget, every steed I sell is covered by my no-quibble, money-back guarantee. Have a safe journey!'

Alexander grunted something and flicked the reins against my rump. I started walking but my mind was in turmoil. How could my master have been so ungrateful? I had helped to make his act the success it was and now he was casting me aside like an old glove. I couldn't believe it, and I told him so.

'I can't believe it,' I said. 'How could you do something like this?'

'I'm doing you a favour,' he said, in that familiar slurred voice. 'Now you won't have to get up every morning and go out to performances. You'll be able to have a nice lie-in.'

'I don't want a lie-in!' I protested. 'I want to work. I mean . . . I do more than just drag this ruddy caravan around. I'm part of the act. Do you think that equine is going to be able to sing your introduction for you? Do you think he'll be able to advise you, as I do?'

Alexander waved a hand in dismissal.

'That sung intro is a bit old-hat now,' he said. 'Josiah tells me that all the best jesters are keeping their routines minimal. You've got to move with the times, Max, no sense in standing still. Look at Jonathan Jolly. He didn't change *his* act and now he's history.'

'I haven't noticed anybody complaining about my intro,' I argued. 'In fact, many people seem to think it's a showstopper! King Cletus loves the song!'

'Yes, but he's heard it plenty of times. I mean, I don't go out there and tell him the same jokes every performance, do I? He'd soon get fed up with that.'

'Well, that's no problem. I can write new lyrics; that's easy for me. In fact, I was toying with some new ideas just the other day. Supposing I came out and sang it more like this . . .'

But in the pause I heard a familiar sound: the long, drawn-out rasps of my master snoring. I felt furious, but my attempts to rouse him from his stupor were fruitless, so there was nothing for it but to plod back across the dark plains in the direction of home.

Chapter 25

A Little Advice

Once there, we went through the usual sorry routine. Mistress Sarah met us with a lantern and proceeded to try and wake Alexander, which was no easy matter. Eventually he stirred himself, half climbed, half fell down from the caravan, muttered a few words of apology to his poor wife and staggered off to bed.

It being a cool night, Mistress Sarah led me and Maximus to the barn, where she was obliged to find some extra food for the new arrival.

'Why on earth did he buy an equine?' she asked me.

I hung my head.

'To replace me,' I said, dismally. 'Somebody convinced him that he was far too grand to be pulled around by a scruffy old buffalope.'

Mistress Sarah's expression hardened.

'Is that so?' she murmured. 'We'll see about that.'

She glanced towards the house.

'I'll speak to him in the morning,' she said. 'There's little point in trying to get through to him in that state.'

'I'm sorry, Mistress,' I said. 'I pleaded with him not to go in that tavern, but he wouldn't listen.'

She stroked my head fondly.

'It's not your fault, Max. You're the one thing around here that I can depend on.'

She threw a doubtful look at Maximus.

'I don't think there's a creature in the world that can take your place – and Alexander would know that too if his brain wasn't addled with drink.'

She bid me goodnight and went into the house, leaving me alone with Maximus, who was poking his nose disdainfully into the food that Mistress Sarah had left out.

'These are lean pickings,' he observed haughtily, using the common language of the plains, though from his mouth it sounded somehow rather well-to-do. 'I hope we don't get this every night.'

I studied him for a moment. Mistress Sarah might have believed that Alexander would find his right mind once he was sober, but I knew how stubborn the man could be when his mind was fixed on something. No, I would need to work on Maximus a bit, just to ensure that events swung back in my favour.

I sidled up alongside him and began to eat.

'The food's generally rather humble around here. Not what you're used to, I'm sure.'

Maximus tossed his head.

'Until recently, I wandered the plains of Neruvia, with thirty fine-looking mares at my beck and call,' he said. 'I ate the lush grasses of the plains, whenever I wanted. Then the Uprights came with their long snake coils.'

'Ropes,' I told him. 'They call them ropes.'

'Whatever. They overpowered me. Let me tell you, it took ten of them to subdue me and a couple of them will never walk again.'

'I don't wonder,' I said. 'You are a magnificent physical specimen.'

Maximus shrugged his huge shoulders.

'I don't like to boast . . .'

Yes you do! I thought.

'. . . but some creatures in this world are just born superior to their fellows. Why, from the earliest age, I was renowned amongst my herd for my exceptional feats of strength, my speed and agility and, of course, my dashing good looks.'

207

'I can see why that would be the case,' I agreed. 'Must be a terrible come-down for you.'

He stopped eating and looked at me.

'What do you mean?' he asked.

'Well, being tethered to the caravan of a lowly jester. I mean, it's nothing to me, I'm a humble . . .' (it almost choked me to say this!) '. . . beast of burden. But you! You were born to carry a King as he rides out to hunt panthers . . . or to bear a Prince across the desert to attend his coronation . . . not to drag a caravan around the lowest, seediest taverns in the land.'

Maximus snorted through his nostrils.

'I'm sorry, but . . . what *is* a jester, exactly? I can see he wears strangely coloured skins, but . . .'

Here was my opening and I took it.

'A jester is a professional idiot,' I said. 'A man who makes his living by falling about, singing, shouting and telling crude jokes. Everywhere he goes, people laugh at him. I mean, you've seen what's written on the side of his caravan, haven't you?'

Maximus shook his head.

'I know nothing of the Upright tongue,' he said.

'Oh, of course not.'

I'd been counting on this.

'Well, basically it says, "See the silly idiot and his equally stupid assistant." That will be you, obviously.

208

And under that it says, "We're so thick, we'll make you wee yourself laughing".'

Maximus flared his nostrils and looked quite affronted.

'Oh dear,' he said. 'That doesn't sound like something I'd want to be associated with.'

'I quite understand,' I said. 'Me, I've got used to all the messing about now.'

'Messing about?'

Maximus was clearly getting rather worried.

'Yes, well, you see, when you pull the caravan, you're part of the act, aren't you? I don't mind wearing the silly hat, so much. But the worst bit is when he invites the audience to throw rotten eggs and fruit at you. It doesn't bother me much with my nice thick coat, but somebody like you now . . .'

'They throw things at you?' cried Maximus. 'Isn't there some kind of a law against that?'

'Apparently not. Oh, and then there's the bit with the sign that he hangs on your tail. It just says, "Kick me!" And you know, the kids in the villages, they can be so rough. My rear end is just one mass of bruises. At least I won't have to suffer that any more.'

Now Maximus was looking nervously around.

'There's clearly been some frightful mistake!' he said. 'I'm not cut out for that kind of treatment!'

'Oh, you'll be all right,' I told him. 'Big strong fellow

like you. You get used to it eventually. At first, it's a bit unnerving, everyone laughing at you and throwing things. . .'

'And kicking you!' added Maximus.

'And kicking you, yes. But you know, we creatures are put on this earth to suffer and I suppose we just have to accept it.'

'Hmmpph!' said Maximus. 'That might be your view, but it's certainly not mine. I'm from very good stock, you know.'

'I can see that.'

'And I'm not used to the ways of commoners.'

'Oh, you'll soon get the hang of it. Let me see now, what's on the agenda for tomorrow?'

I pretended to think for a moment.

'Oh yes, of course . . . the village of Much Grunting In The Marsh. Delightful place. The people there are . . . what's the word? Homely. Yes, they may be filthy and they may smell like a cesspit in high summer, but they know how to make you feel welcome. Of course, since they had the pestilence there, you've got to be careful not to actually *touch* them, but . . .'

'The pestilence?'

Maximus was looking anxiously towards the exit, but Mistress Sarah had closed up the barn doors for the night.

'Oh yes, but don't worry, it's not a particularly bad one. More akin to leprosy, really. You don't die, but bits of you tend to go rotten and drop off.'

Now Maximus's eyes got very wide and he looked at me in total panic.

'Look, this isn't right! You've got to help me get out of here!'

I shook my head.

'No chance of that, I'm afraid. Mistress Sarah keeps the doors locked in case of lupers. Loads of them around here; sometimes they're all over this place like a rash. But tomorrow morning, my master will come for you and he'll get you ready for your visit. He'll have the hat and the sign for your tail . . . and, of course, he'll administer some protection for your trip to Much Grunting In The Marsh.'

'P . . . p . . . protection?' gasped Maximus.

'Oh yes, nothing to worry about. An old folk remedy that seems to work. What he'll do, he'll insert a big lump of cow dung up each of your nostrils and then he'll sew them shut. It stings a bit, but it's over in moments and, let's face it, it's better than going down with the pestilence, isn't it?'

Early the following morning, my master came to let us out. I'd had a bit of warning that he was on his

211

way because, even at such a distance, I'd been able to hear the shouting of Mistress Sarah, followed by the crashing of plates and pans as they were hurled around the interior of the house.

After a short interval, I heard the sounds of my master's footsteps approaching the barn and then the doors swung open – and Alexander was knocked flying by Maximus as he galloped out of there at full speed.

Alexander lay in the mud for a moment and then groaned. He lifted a hand to his head and it was quite clear that he was feeling very much the worse for wear. He stared blearily along the track, but Maximus was already a small black dot on the horizon, trailing a cloud of dust in his wake. My master got painfully back to his feet and hobbled into the barn.

'What do you suppose got into him?' he asked suspiciously.

'I've no idea,' I said. 'Mind you, he was a nervy type. Didn't like being shut up the barn, not one bit. Do you think we should go and look for him, Master?'

Alexander glanced back towards the house, then shook his head.

'Forget him,' he said. 'It was a stupid idea, anyway. Come on, we'd better get going.'

Chapter 26

Exciting News

We settled back into our regular routine. My master would behave himself for a while, would be the very model of a sober citizen; then, something would happen to weaken his resolve; a chance encounter with an old friend, a skirmish with some brigands on the road, a particularly troublesome audience that just wouldn't laugh in all the right places . . . The excuses varied but the results were always the same. A night spent in the tavern drinking as though his very life depended upon it. I began to realise that my master spent quite a bit of time looking for reasons to start drinking again, and that his problems went deeper than I had at first imagined.

And then I began to notice that something about Mistress Sarah had changed. She didn't look any different and she didn't really behave differently, but there was some subtle thing about the way she carried herself, the way she would look away and smile when I was talking to her, that made me think that she knew something I didn't. She had a secret and, I felt sure, it was something good.

One day, on the road to our latest appearance, at a big archery tournament, I even asked the master about it.

'Have you noticed anything different about Mistress Sarah?' I asked him.

'How do you mean?' he muttered.

'Well, I can't quite put my hoof on it, but there's definitely something going on with her. She's been behaving a bit oddly.'

Alexander considered this news for a moment.

'I can't say that I've been taking a lot of notice of her recently,' he said. 'I'm always so busy. What sort of thing do you mean?'

'Well, she seems to be happy all the time . . . smiling . . . and I can't help feeling that there's something going on that she's not telling anybody else about. I'm sure of it.'

Alexander suddenly seemed very serious.

'You . . . you don't think .. ?'

'What, Master?'

'That she's . . . *seeing* somebody?'

'Seeing somebody?' I echoed. I must confess I was bewildered by this question. 'I expect she sees lots of people.'

'You know what I mean,' he said. 'You don't think . . . well. That she could be having an affair?'

'Is that like a party or something?'

'No, you idiot! It means being romantic with another person.'

'Oh, I see.'

I thought about it for a moment.

'I suppose she has every opportunity,' I said. 'I mean, we're out nearly every day, aren't we? And who could blame her if she did seek companionship elsewhere? I mean, the way you carry on . . .'

'What's that supposed to mean?' protested Alexander.

'Well, the drinking and everything . . .'

He made a sound of exasperation.

'It would be nice, Max, if, just for once, you didn't use every little thing that happens as an opportunity to give me a lecture about my evil ways.'

'Master, I was only saying . . .'

'Never mind! Turn around.'

'What?'

'You heard me! Turn around. We're going back to the house.'

'But . . . what about the tournament?'

'Never mind that. They'll just have to wait for us, won't they? This is something that needs to be sorted out, right now.'

I did as I was told, but I couldn't help feeling he was jumping to conclusions.

'Master, I only said that there was something *different* about her. You're the one who came up with this half-baked theory about a romance.'

'Yes, but it makes sense, doesn't it? I mean, she's left to her own devices all day long, she's nothing to occupy her time and, let's face it, she's an attractive young woman. Any man who saw her would be interested.'

'Possibly . . . but I'm sure she isn't the sort to go and do something like that.'

'She's a *woman*, Max; who can ever fathom what goes on in their heads?'

'Even so, I really think you need to . . .'

'Just get a move on!' he snapped.

I could tell from the tone of his voice that he was not going to change his mind on this one.

I covered the short distance to the homestead in record time, thinking that, if I picked up the pace a bit, we might still make it back to the tournament without too much delay. But, as we moved along the dirt track that led to the house, I was dismayed to see an unfamiliar carriage, drawn by two equines, standing at the front of the house. Alexander noticed it too.

'Whose carriage is that?' he asked me.

'I'm sure I don't know,' I told him.

'My suspicions were right,' he growled and his voice fairly simmered with anger. 'She's been seeing some-body behind my back!'

'Master, I'm sure she wouldn't do that!' I cried. 'There's probably a very good explanation for that carriage being here. Maybe . . . maybe it's a workman come to make repairs.'

'I doubt it,' said Alexander coldly. And I heard the hiss of steel as he drew his curved sword from its sheath.

'Now hold on a moment,' I warned him. 'Let's not be too hasty.'

We drew to a halt behind the carriage and, at that very instant, the front door opened and somebody stepped out.

Alexander gave a gasp of surprise and I must confess, I was a bit shocked myself; for the man who had just emerged into the sunlight was a skinny old fellow with thinning grey hair and a long beard. He was wearing an expensive silk cloak and, in one hand, he carried a leather bag. He turned in shocked surprise as Alexander jumped down from the caravan and strode menacingly towards him, sword held ready to attack.

'Who are you?' snarled Alexander. 'What are you doing in my home?'

The old man's eyes got very big and he began to back away from Alexander.

'Please,' he gasped. 'Put down that sword!'

'Not until you tell me what you are doing in my house.'

'I . . . I came to visit your wife!' gasped the old man, pointing a gnarled finger at the open door.

'You admit it? As brazen as that?'

The old man looked confused.

'Of course, Sir, it was your wife who contacted me. She *asked* me to come . . .'

'She *what*?'

Alexander lunged forward and, grabbing the man by one shoulder, he held the razor-sharp sword against his skinny throat.

'And why exactly would my young wife wish to spend time with an old rascal like you?' he roared.

'I . . . I visit many women,' croaked the old man. 'My skills are renowned.'

'Your . . . skills? Skills at what? You old blackguard, I've a mind to slit you open and spill your entrails!'

Now the old fellow was terrified.

'Don't do that, sir, I beseech you! I'd prefer to keep my entrails where they belong, if you don't mind. I mean no harm, I simply offer a service to women like your wife; I'm only making an honest living!'

Now my master looked really shocked.

'You mean to tell me . . . they *pay* you?'

'Yes, sir, a reasonable sum, nothing more. I do not overcharge, I can assure you. If you would like to look at my accounting book, you'll see that I charge every woman the same fee!'

My poor master now looked as though he had been clouted over the head with a heavy object.

'Well, that's really noble of you,' he murmured. 'But nevertheless, I'm afraid I am going to have to hurt you, very badly.'

'Alexander!'

The voice came from the open doorway and we all turned our heads to see Mistress Sarah standing there, an expression of horror on her face.

'What are you doing?' she cried.

He glared at her.

'I'm telling your aging boyfriend that he has made a very big mistake coming here today.'

'My . . . *boyfriend*?'

Mistress Sarah stared at her husband for a moment and then her expression changed, to one of amusement.

She began to chuckle, softly at first, but with mounting volume, until she had to throw back her head and laugh out loud.

'Oh, you think its funny, do you?' cried Alexander. 'You think it's a laugh, seeing another man when your husband's back is turned? Well, forgive me if I don't share your amusement! We'll see if you're still laughing when I slit this old buzzard open!'

'Alexander, you idiot! He's not my boyfriend . . . he's a doctor. Doctor Zacchariah. I asked him to come here to examine me.'

Alexander released his grip on the old man and moved quickly across to his wife.

'You . . . you are ill?' he gasped. 'Why didn't you tell me?'

She shook her head.

'No, I'm not ill. I've never felt better, especially after what the doctor has just told me.'

'What are you talking about?' cried Alexander.

'Can't you guess?' Mistress Sarah smiled enchantingly. 'It's finally happened, Alexander. I'm going to have a baby.'

I don't think I'd seen my master more humbled than he was that day. He must have apologised to Doctor Zachariah about twenty times before he managed to get the old man back into his carriage and away from there. Then he and Mistress Sarah went into the house to talk, while I waited patiently outside.

At length, Alexander and Mistress Sarah came back out, all smiles, and they kissed and hugged goodbye, before Alexander vaulted back up onto the seat and urged me to make all haste back to the tournament.

'We can't afford to miss a performance now,' he told me. 'There'll soon be another mouth to feed!'

I did as I was bid and retraced my steps across the plains with as much speed as I could muster.

'I told you there must be a reasonable explanation!' I shouted back over my shoulder.

'You did and you were right!' he shouted back. 'I can't tell you how delighted I am, Max. We'd just about given up all hope of ever having a child and now it's confirmed.'

'Will the baby be along any day now?' I asked.

'Not for ages. A woman carries a child for the best part of a year.'

'That long?'

I was surprised. Back in the herd, a Mother buffalope would carry a calf for only a few moons before she gave birth to it.

'The time will soon go,' he assured me. 'Meanwhile,

221

we must do everything we can to make sure that my child will want for nothing.'

He was silent for a moment and then he said, 'There are going to have to be some changes.'

'What kind of changes, Master? You want me to work harder?'

He laughed.

'I didn't mean you, Max. No, I'm talking about myself. The drinking and all that. It's going to have to stop, once and for all.'

'Yes, Master,' I said, but I must confess I didn't really believe that he would manage to keep his word.

But I was wrong. From that day forward Alexander Darke was a changed man. He never so much as looked at a tavern again. Even his old cronies like The Great Sensimo couldn't entice him to accompany them. It was as though he had seen some kind of light and had been cured of his habits, overnight.

Meanwhile, the two of us worked as hard as we could and Alexander began to put away some money after each performance, which he kept in a wooden chest in a secret place that only he knew of.

And, just as he had predicted, the time passed quickly. Mistress Sarah's shape began to change, gradually at first but more and more dramatically until she was waddling around, with a great round bump where her middle used to be.

And then my master started saying, 'It won't be long now', and I could tell how excited he was at the prospect of being a father. He kept reminding me that when the time finally came, I was to race into Jerebim, where I would seek out and bring back Old Megs, the midwife, who would help to bring the new baby into the world.

As the last days slipped by, I could feel my own excitement mounting. I sensed that this baby would be important to me for many reasons. After all, he or she would be a Darke – and I had given my life to the Darke family after their kindness towards me.

But all that was to come. For now, there was just the joy of knowing that soon, a child would be born, and that I would be there to share the excitement.

Chapter 27

A New Arrival

It was a particularly turbulent morning, I remember, the sky piled with great banks of tumbling cloud. A surprisingly brisk wind was gusting in off the plains and the high-pitched sound it made was enough to set your nerves jangling.

It being so close to the estimated birth date, my master had stopped taking any bookings and the two of us were left to kick our heels around the place, waiting for something to happen. But, annoyingly, nothing did. Mistress Sarah waddled around the place, perfectly calm and content, and she got so fed up with my master following her around the house, looking concerned, that she sent him out to me to get him from 'under her feet'.

'Go and work on some new routines,' she urged us. 'I'll come and get you if I need you.'

So the two of us retired to the barn where we tried to work on some new material.

'Right, Max, let's see what you think of this one,' said Alexander.

He was fond of trying out his new material on me and little wonder, given my ability to recognise a winning joke when I heard it.

'A man walks into a tavern leading a luper on a length of rope. The landlord is horrified. "Take that thing out of here, it's dangerous!" he cries. "No it's not," says the man, "it's trained."'

'Master, you cannot train a luper. Those things are quite mad, anyone can tell you that.'

'Yes, well, that's exactly what the landlord says. "You cannot train a luper, they're quite mad!" So the man says, "Watch this!" He opens the luper's jaws and places one hand in between the creature's teeth . . .'

'Oh, goodness, Master, is the man insane?'

'No, he's not! He just believes that the luper is trained enough not to hurt him.'

'Well, you wouldn't catch me doing a stupid thing like that, even if I *had* a hand to put in there.'

'Shush. Now, with his *other* hand, the man picks up a clay jug from the bar top and with one swift move-ment, he smashes it over the luper's head.'

'Oh, that's his hand gone, then.'

PHILIP CAVENEY

'No it's not! He withdraws his hand and there's not a scratch on it. Well, you can imagine! Amazement from everyone! Then the man looks around the crowded tavern and says, "Would anybody else like to try that?" And this fool standing at the bar says, "I'll have a go, but please don't hit me with a jug."'

Silence.

'Er . . . I'm sorry?' I said. 'I don't get it. Why would the man hit the fool when he's got his hand in a luper's mouth?'

'No, you misunderstand. The fool thought the man wanted him to put his hand in *his* mouth.'

'But why would the man put his hand in his own mouth and then hit the fool with a jug?'

'NO! The fool thought the man wanted the fool to bite his hand.'

'Oh, well I suppose it's understandable, hitting somebody with a jug when he's biting your hand.'

'But he's not biting the hand, is he?'

'Is he not? But you just said . . .'

'I said that for convenience, but it's not what I meant. When I say, "biting" the hand, I really mean *not* biting the hand.'

'Then . . . why . . . ?'

'You're deliberately not getting it!'

226

'I'm not deliberately not getting it. There's nothing deliberate about it. I'm just not getting it.'

Alexander sighed.

'Let me explain,' he said. 'The fool thought the man wanted the fool to put his teeth around the man's hand, without biting him, but the fool also thought that the man wanted to clout the fool with a clay jug, just as he did the luper.'

'Oh . . . I see.'

'Well?'

'It's not very funny, is it? Perhaps if the man hit the luper with a jug, the luper could bite off his hand and the man could say, "I told you he was 'armless!"'

'That's not funny!' protested Alexander. 'And anyway . . . he wouldn't be armless, would he? He'd be *hand*less and that's not quite the same thing.'

I thought about it for a moment and then my rapier-like wit kicked in.

'Well, maybe the man could turn to the landlord and say, "Give me a hand to get this luper out of here!"'

'No, that's too obvious! Can't you see that the original joke is based on a misunderstanding?'

'I'm not surprised. I certainly misunderstood it.'

'Yes, but that's because you . . .'

My master broke off in surprise as Mistress Sarah appeared at the open door of the barn. She had a hand on her swollen stomach and, though she was still smiling, there was something decidedly strained about her expression.

'Alexander,' she said, calmly. 'It's time.'

'Yes, dear,' said Alexander, waving a hand in dismissal. 'Just put the food on the table and I'll be in just as soon as I've explained something to old thicko here.'

'No dear, you don't understand. It's not time for food. It's *time*.'

My master looked at her for a moment and then he did a passable impression of a man waking up from a deep sleep. His eyes widened until they were nearly bulging out of his head.

'Oh,' he said. 'Oh it's *time*!'

He looked at me. 'Max, it's time!'

He jumped to his feet and began to panic.

'It's time! Time! Max, don't just stand there! Go for the . . . the . . .'

'The what, Master?'

'That old woman, the . . . whatever she calls herself.'

'The . . . midwife, Master?'

'Yes, her! Get over to Jerebim as fast as you can and bring her here. Don't take no for an answer!'

Now he ran across to his wife.

'Are you all right?' he asked her. 'Are you in pain?

228

Is there anything you need me to do? I don't know what to do!'

'I'm fine,' she assured him. 'Help me back to the house and we'll get everything ready for Old Megs.'

'Yes, of course.'

Alexander shot a look at me.

'Are you still here?' he cried. 'Get a move on!'

'Yes, Master!'

I didn't wait to be told again. I headed out of the barn and raced along the track leading to the open plains. I kept my head down and went as fast as my legs could carry me and, even though it was a fair old distance, I didn't stop until I had reached my destination.

Old Megs lived in a ramshackle house in the poorest part of the town. On first inspection, it looked as though scores of other people lived in there with her, as there were lots of men and women wandering in and out of the open doorway. Half a dozen filthy, bedraggled urchins were playing in the dirt in the front yard.

'I'm looking for Old Megs,' I told them, as I approached. The response was gales of laughter from the children. Clearly they'd never seen a talking buffalope before.

'You're funny,' shrieked one of them, a filthy little

boy of perhaps six years with a shaved head and a mouthful of rotting teeth. 'You've got a funny face!'

I regarded him with a certain look.

'Yours isn't much to write home about, either,' I assured him. 'Now, tell me, where is Old Megs?'

'She's having a lie-down,' said an equally mucky little girl. 'She's been at the ale again.'

'What?'

I was horrified by this news.

'Well, go and get her up, immediately. This is an emergency, a matter of life and death!'

They didn't seem at all impressed by this information, so I added:

'There's money involved.'

That did the trick. The rotten-toothed boy jumped up and ran into the house as though he had just been prodded up the backside with a red hot poker. A few moments later, the shutters of an upstairs window opened and Old Megs leaned out, looking distinctly the worse for wear. Mind you, she wasn't much to look at in her best condition.

She was a filthy, wizened crone of advanced years, with a great wart-ridden hooked nose, grey sunken cheeks and, as far as I could tell, not one tooth in her head. Her long grey hair hung down to her shoulders and age had bent her back, but her tiny grey eyes were shrewd enough and her skills as a midwife were renowned throughout Jerebim. A lot of people thought she was a witch and they probably weren't far from the truth.

'What d'you want?' she croaked, in a voice as dry as the plains during a drought.

'You,' I said. 'I've been sent by Alexander Darke, who bids you come to the aid of his young wife who is about to have her first baby.'

She shrugged her humped shoulders.

'Well, you'll have to wait a while,' she said. 'I've been drinking and I need to sleep it off.'

'Drinking?' I cried. 'It's barely midday!'

'Can't help that. I lanced a boil for somebody this morning and he paid me with a barrel of home-brewed ale. Well, it needed drinking, before some of the little mice around here got their paws on it.'

She directed an accusing look down at the urchins below her.

'Never mind about that!' I cried, trying not to think too much about the implications of little children drinking strong ale. 'You must come with me, immediately,' I said. 'This is an emergency!'

'Oh, I doubt that. A lot of young women seem to think that their baby is the most important child ever conceived, but it's usually just panic. She can wait till tonight.'

I glared up at her.

'Let me assure you, madam, that she will not. My master paid you a handsome advance to attend this birth, did he not?'

She nodded.

'Well, yes . . .'

'So unless you want me to start taking this filthy hovel apart with my bare horns, you'd better get your decrepit body down here right now. Do I make myself clear?'

I know this was uncharacteristically aggressive of me but, in my defence, this was a desperate situation.

Old Megs muttered something under her breath that I didn't quite catch, but I doubt that she was complimenting me on my persistence. She slammed the shutters and, a few moments later, she appeared at the door, wearing a filthy cloak and carrying a rusa skin bag. She came stomping over to me and, close up, I could smell the powerful alcohol fumes coming off her.

'It's disgraceful,' I observed. 'Somebody with your responsibility should exercise a little more self-control.'

'Oh, pipe down, goody four-shoes,' she grunted.

Then she looked quickly around.

'Where's the carriage?' she asked.

'Carriage? What carriage?'

She glared at me.

'Well, how am I to get to the Darke's residence? You want me to walk?'

'I doubt that you *could* in your state,' I told her. 'Here, climb up on my back.'

She looked at me.

'You are jesting, I hope.'

'No, I leave that kind of thing to my master. Now stop wasting time, and climb on.'

I lowered myself onto my knees in order to assist her and with much grumbling and complaining, she got her wiry little body astride me. I eased myself back to my feet.

'Are you sitting comfortably?' I asked her.

'Fairly,' she said, but she didn't sound so sure about it.

'Good. Now, hang on tight,' I advised her.

'Very well, but heed me, Master Buffalope, I am old and frail, so please don't go too arrrrrrrrgggghhh-hhhh!'

I paid no attention to her after that. I was too intent on getting back to the homestead and, for her part, she must have hung on tenaciously enough, because she didn't fall off, not once, and then there we were, out of the town and racing across the open plains, heading for home.

Chapter 28

Don't Stop Me Now!

It was all going suspiciously well. I was just complimenting myself on a job well done, when I heard Old Megs shout a warning and, lifting my head, I saw them: a band of Neruvian hunters, some ten or twelve of them in all, mounted on equines and armed to the teeth. They were on the road ahead, riding straight towards us at speed.

'Neruvians!' screeched Old Megs, just in case I'd failed to notice. 'They're the worst kind of brigands. We must turn back!'

'We can't do that!' I shouted back. 'My mistress needs help.'

I knew enough about these scavengers of the plains to realise that buffalope were common currency to them and I was also aware that they wouldn't let a little old lady get in their way. She'd be dead in an instant and

I would be a prisoner, heading back to some camp out on the plains, ready to be sold to the highest bidder. I had lived through that experience once and I did not intend to suffer through it again. Furthermore, Mistress Sarah couldn't afford the time it would take for me to try and elude them. So I simply quickened my pace.

'Press yourself down flat,' I shouted.

Old Megs did as she was told, but not without shouting out a whole heap of abuse at me.

'What do you think you're doing? You stupid idiot buffalope; you'll get us both killed! Turn back now, before it's too late.'

'You tend to your midwifery and leave the manly stuff to me,' I said, with a calmness that surprised me.

I maintained my speed, noticing as I did so that a couple of the hunters were reaching for their ropes, clearly with the intention of lassoing me.

They had, no doubt, expected me to veer to one side in an attempt to escape them and for the moment, that was exactly what I pretended to do. But I had another plan. At the last possible moment, I swung back to face them and aimed myself at the closest of the Neruvians, a big ugly shaven-headed thug with tattoos all over his face.

I put my head down and ran full tilt into the man's equine, my horns striking it full in the chest. There was an impact that shook me from head to foot and I felt a momentary sadness at having to treat another four-legged creature so brutally; but then the equine was rearing upwards into the air as though it had taken flight and its rider was screaming in terror. The first equine slammed into the one behind it, smashing it aside and the two creatures went rolling in the dust, taking their luckless riders with them.

Then I was past them and racing on down the dirt road. I could hear old Megs jabbering away behind me, what sounded like a prayer, but I didn't dare slow down to ask if she was all right.

I hoped I had gained us some respite but, only a few moments later, Old Megs yelled that the riders were coming after us. I risked a glance over my shoulder and saw that they were spurring their mounts and pursuing me with renewed vigour, fanning themselves out behind me in a ragged line.

Very well, I thought, *if that's how you want to play it . . .*

Every time I glanced back it was to discover that the Neruvians' fleet-footed mounts were rapidly gaining on me; I knew in my heart that I could not maintain this breakneck pace for ever. Then a lasso came snaking through the air, as somebody tried to drop a noose around my neck. But I twisted my head to one side and the loop snagged against one of my horns, then pulled tight. I quickened my pace to take up any slack and then judging my moment, I jerked my head hard to one side.

There was a muffled exclamation from behind me, followed by a thud. Suddenly, I could feel that I was pulling extra weight and glancing back, I saw that the Neruvian had been jerked clear out of his saddle and was now ploughing a furrow in the dust with his nose. Judging by the noise he was making, he wasn't enjoying the experience very much, but he must have had the rope looped around his wrist and could not let go.

'Old Megs!' I bellowed. 'You must cut that rope.'

'With what?' she screamed back. 'My teeth?'

'I don't care how you do it,' I assured her. 'But he's slowing us down.'

'Just a moment.'

She was rummaging in her midwife's bag and after a few moments, she must have found a sharp implement, because she began sawing frantically at the rope. I was aware now that two riders had come up, one on either side of me, and glancing left and right, I saw that both men had resorted to pulling out their bows and arrows. Now that I had injured some of their comrades, they no longer cared if I lived or died. I desperately needed to put on more speed, but the screaming, flailing figure lurching through the dust behind me was slowing me down no end.

'Hurry!' I urged Old Megs.

'I'm doing my best,' she shrieked.

'Do better!'

Now the riders on either side of me were pulling back their bows and taking aim. They had me in a deadly crossfire, aiming at my unprotected flanks . . .

There was a sudden twang and the rope parted. Set free from the drag of the fallen rider, I shot suddenly forward, just as the two riders released their respective bowstrings. I was dimly aware of something flashing past inches from my rear end and then there were two screams as the arrows found human targets instead of their intended one.

'Incredible!' shrieked Old Megs. 'You made them shoot each other.'

'Of course!' I gasped. 'All part of my . . . cunning plan.'

Not that it was, of course, just a happy accident, but she didn't need to know that.

And now I was encountering another problem. Going along at such a frantic pace was rapidly getting the better of me. I could hardly draw breath and there were still at least six Neruvians in pursuit. I could not hope to outrun them any longer. Glancing back, I saw that the remaining riders had dropped back a little, to see if they could help their fallen comrades, but now they were coming on again, intent on vengeance. I slewed round, coming to a halt, and throwing up a great cloud of dust.

'What are you doing?' gasped Old Megs.

'Climb down,' I told her. 'Quickly.'

'But they are heavily armed,' she said.

'Climb down now, or go into the battle with me,' I said. 'It's your choice.'

That seemed to do the trick. She clambered off my back and moved off a short distance, clutching her cloak tightly around her as though she was cold. I gathered all my strength and pawed the ground a little, gathering my strength watching as the riders warily approached me. They all had their bows out now, any thought of taking me alive abandoned.

A strange kind of calm settled over me. I drew a bead on the closest of the riders and then I launched myself forward. As I ran, I remembered back to my Father's brave charge against hunters like these, when I was just a little calf, and I hoped that my efforts would not end as tragically as his. Even as I thought it, an arrow slammed against my shoulder, but glanced off bone and went spinning away. I didn't slow my pace, even when a second arrow buried itself deep in the flesh of my neck. I just kept running and then I was in amongst the riders and I was dealing out my own vengeance, thinking as I did so of my parents and the terrible things that had happened to them.

My head seemed to fill with a hot red mist and I moved instinctively, swinging my horns from side to side, lunging, kicking, throwing my weight this way and that and, with every movement, I felt a weight pushed backwards or sideways or upwards. My head filled with the bellow of terrified equines, the grunts and curses of stricken men, and I was only dimly aware of hard-edged weapons that slashed and stabbed and tore, but I felt no pain.

And then, quite suddenly, my horns were finding nothing but empty air and I stopped moving and let the redness recede. I looked quickly around me, and saw that, aside from Old Megs, I was the only creature left standing on the plain. All around me were dead or maimed men and animals, some lying still, some moaning and trying to crawl away. I stood for a moment, wanting to be sure that nobody was going to come after me again, but it didn't take long to establish that none of them was capable of doing that.

So I turned and walked back to Old Megs, who just stood there staring at me with new respect in her eyes.

'I believe that was the bravest thing I ever saw,' she told me.

'You should have seen my Father,' I said; and I felt my eyes filling with tears.

'You're wounded,' she said. 'Let me take a look. I have salves in my bag.'

I shook my head.

'No time for that,' I said. 'Mistress Sarah is waiting. Come, climb up onto my back, we still have quite a way to go.'

She didn't argue with me this time. She did as she was told and I set off again, leaving what was left of the Neruvians in the dust behind me.

Chapter 29

A New Beginning

There were no more incidents on the road back to the homestead and, before very much longer, we arrived safely and I was able to discharge my passenger, who bowed her ancient head and hobbled meekly into the house; then there was nothing for me to do, but go back to waiting.

After a little while, my master came out to join me, saying that Old Megs had banned him from the room because he kept asking stupid questions. Then he noticed the arrow sticking out of my neck.

'Max, what happened?' he gasped.

'Oh, just an encounter with a few Neruvians,' I said. 'They wanted to stop me from coming home. But I managed to persuade them to let us go by.'

He regarded the blood and equine hair clotted on my horns and shook his head.

'Looks like they needed a lot of persuasion,' he said. 'Come on, let's get that arrow out of you.'

He led me to the barn, fetched hot water and a sharp knife and set to work digging out the arrowhead. He kept apologising for the pain he was causing me, and I have to tell you, it *was* pretty painful, but my thoughts were on what was happening in the house. I hoped that Mistress Sarah would be all right and that it hadn't taken me too long to bring back Old Megs.

'So tell me about these Neruvians,' said Alexander, as he worked. 'Were there many of them?'

'Not so very many,' I said. 'Maybe ten or twelve. I didn't take an awful lot of notice.'

I looked at him.

'I don't think I've ever told you this, but when you first found me, it was Neruvians I was running from then. They . . . killed my Father and took my Mother captive.'

He lifted his eyebrows.

'How is it you've never mentioned it before?' he asked me.

I shrugged my shoulders, sending a fresh spasm of pain through the wound in my neck.

'I suppose when it had just happened, my human tongue wasn't up to telling you the story. And then later, when I had learned how to speak to you, I didn't much feel like talking about it.'

He stroked my head fondly.

'You must have had every reason to turn around and run,' he said. 'But you didn't. You truly are a remarkable creature, Max.'

'I have my moments,' I admitted.

I kept thinking we might be interrupted by a call from the house, but my master soon had the wound cleaned and dressed and still there was nothing.

The light gradually went out of the day and the night descended. The storm that had been threatening since morning finally found its voice and great rolls of thunder crashed over the distant hills. Forked lightning came stabbing down at the cringing earth, momentarily lighting up the plains all around us and still we waited, until it seemed that nothing was ever going to happen, and then, quite unexpectedly, between the rolls of thunder, we heard a different sound: a tiny, puling cry, coming from somewhere in the house.

We looked at each other and I saw that my master's face held an expression of absolute joy. I don't think I had ever seen him so happy and, I'm sorry to say, I never saw him that happy ever again. Sometimes, when I close my eyes, I can picture his face, still frozen in that expression of perfect happiness.

He stood like that for just a moment and then he turned and ran into the house.

I waited, pacing anxiously up and down by the open doorway, and it seemed that another age passed before I saw or heard anything.

And then finally . . . finally, Alexander came out of the house and he was holding a little wrapped bundle in his arms and I saw that there were tears in his eyes. For an instant, I felt a stab of anxiety, because I thought that something terrible had happened, that there was something wrong with the baby. But then I saw that he was smiling and I realised that what I could see in his eyes were tears of joy. He came up to me and held the bundle out so I could see it.

'I can only show you for a moment,' he said. 'And then he must go back to his Mother.'

'He?' I whispered.

'Yes. A boy. A good, strong boy.'

I looked into the blanket and I saw a tiny face looking out at me, a pale face with two dark eyes and a tangle of jet black hair. I could see that the baby's ears were pointed. As I looked, his little pink mouth curved into a smile and I knew at that moment, that the two of us were going to be the best of friends, the closest of allies. In that very instant, we bonded and I knew that I would happily lay down my own life to protect this new child; that I would pay the ultimate price to keep him from harm.

'Oh, Master,' I said. 'He's beautiful.'

'Isn't he, though?' Alexander was beaming, full of pride. 'He looks like me, don't you think?'

'Well . . .'

I didn't want to tell him that the child looked exactly like his mother, but the truth was, at that moment, he did. If she had spat him out of her mouth, he couldn't have looked more like her. But I tried to break the news gently.

'He has his Mother's eyes and ears,' I said. 'But I think the nose is definitely yours, Master. And the . . . the . . . '

A tiny hand came into view, gesticulating at me, as though giving me a hint.

'The *fingers*,' I said. 'You can see that they're exactly like yours.'

'The fingers. Yes.'

Luckily, Alexander was so delighted, it seemed he could be fobbed off with just about anything.

'A boy,' he repeated. 'I'll be able to teach him the sword. And my jester's routine, of course. I can see him now, standing on a stage, telling his jokes and riddles. He'll be able to carry on the Darke tradition when I'm gone.'

He glanced at me.

'By the way, we've decided to call him . . .'

'Yes, Master?' I said delightedly.

'Sebastian,' he said. 'After his late grandfather,'

And he turned away and strolled back into the house.

'What . . . not Max?' I whispered.

But there was nobody to hear me say it and, upon reflection, I told myself that I couldn't expect anything else. After all, who would name a child after a silly old buffalope? A ridiculous notion. But, just for a moment there, I had thought . . .

Ah well, it doesn't pay to dwell on regrets. That gets you nowhere. If there's one thing I've learned in all my years of experience, it's that.

The thing is that I now had a new ally and, in years to come, the two of us would go on to have many great adventures together, adventures that will be recounted elsewhere by better storytellers than I.

So . . . it would seem that my tale is told. I am an old buffalope now. My strength is gone, my eyesight is failing and it won't be so long before I go to the great wallow in the sky to be with those who have gone before me. I will see my parents again. I will see Betty and Luthor and maybe old Brutus.

I will not be sad to part. I have led a long and full

life and I have known high adventure and the friend-ship of those who love me.

And in the end, what more can any buffalope ask? Except perhaps, for the occasional barrel of fresh, ripe pommers.

Well, you've got to have a few perks in life, haven't you?